Bitter Night Sweet Dawn

Bitter Night Sweet Dawn

JANET BEDLY

LIFEJOURNEY BOOKS
David C. Cook Publishing Co.
Elgin, Illinois • Weston, Ontario
Nova Distribution Ltd., Torquay, England

Life Journey Books is an imprint of David C. Cook Publishing Co.
David C. Cook Publishing Co., Elgin, Illinois 60120
David C. Cook Publishing Co., Weston, Ontario
Nova Distribution Ltd., Newton Abbot, England

BITTER NIGHT, SWEET DAWN

Cover design by Koechel, Peterson, and Associates, Inc.
First Printing, 1992
Printed in the United States of America
96 95 94 93 92 5 4 3 2 1

Library of Congress Cataloging-in-Publication Data
Bitter Night, Sweet Dawn/Janet Q. Bedley.
p. cm.
ISBN: 0-7814-0942-X
I. Title.
PS3552.E316M37 1992
813'.54—dc20 92-10229
CIP

This is a work of fiction. The story of Maryetta Cobbet is the author's invention. Any resemblance to persons living or dead is purely coincidental with the exception of prominent historical characters and places associated with mid-nineteenth century life and events.

Dedicated with gratitude to
Andre and Anne Marie Lannoo

ACKNOWLEDGMENTS

It is with gratitude that I express my thanks to all who have made this book possible:

Marguerite Armerding, Secretary to Bernie May with Wycliffe, for introducing me to Belgium's Andre and Anne Marie Lannoo.

Andre and Anne Marie Lannoo for their tireless efforts to acquaint me with the history of Belgium, the clothing, the characteristics of the people, and the mid-nineteenth century setting in which the story is placed.

Monsieur Joseph Marinkovich for his assistance with the French language.

Cecile Pimental for digging into Newburyport's development, especially the train stations of that city. She is a librarian there.

Blue's Jay's courteous librarians for always being willing to find the research book I needed—Jill Dessaux and Barbara Martinez.

Jennifer Hoos who first critiqued the manuscript; Gene Bedley, who never stopped encouraging; and Robert Bedley, Sr. for his enduring patience.

1

THE GENTLE SLOPES OF THE RICH IOWA TILL LANDS WERE already taking on the shadows of twilight, and silhouetted trees marked the horizon. Stalks of late July corn were darkly outlined against a burned-out painted skyline. Davenport soil was good. Crops grew like Jack's beanstalk, and the place was growing rapidly with frontiersmen arriving daily from the East.

With the promise for all of such bounty, the natural-born avarice in a man could be easily choked out. Here, beyond the Mississippi, frontier ethics were different from the East. Pioneers understood one another. Each shared a brotherly concern for his neighbor as well as a determination to survive. Ira Cobbet liked that.

The respected son of a recognized surgeon and the brother of several physicians, he had early established a good medical practice back East. He had married and brought his young wife, June, to the Knickerbocker State, where they had lived in one of the finest communities of upstate New York and enjoyed the luxuries of successful professionals.

There Ira had surrounded himself with a coterie of businessmen, the group boasting a good number of Washington politicians. They came often to social gatherings and spoke of the growing tension between the North and the South and the expanding borders of the country. At first the conversations had centered around well-known facts, but later talk had increased about the cattle towns, the stagecoach trails, the freight lines, the pony express, and the obvious need for a railroad beyond the Mississippi. It seemed the politicians were already privy to the proposed routes the tracks would take—and more than a little proud to be in possession of such knowledge.

"If a man had any brains at all, he could make himself a fortune. Of course he'd have to have some idea of the location where the lines would run," announced one guest . . . and Ira walked right into the trap.

His interest in the Western expansion of the country seemed to grow until he spoke of little else. Most of his New York land holdings went on the auction block, as well as many of his wife's treasured family possessions. To invest in the country's future, they would need every dollar they could raise. Thus he had reasoned and gradually convinced June that their future depended on getting in early on the government land grants, buying up as much as possible while the price was still one dollar and twenty-five cents an acre.

JUNE COBBET HAD BEEN born and raised in a small New England town and, though not a member of the gentry, she had never known the extreme hardships she was now experiencing. More than once she wondered if her strength would hold out. Many times in the sweat of ninety-degree days she longed for the East, where always at eventide an ocean breeze might steal in over the land. She wished she had not been so anxious to follow after her strong young husband, nor pampered his enthusiasm for adventure. And for all of Ira's academic prowess, she had now and then found herself wishing he had some down-east horse sense.

When their child was born, together they decided she should be named after both grandmothers, Mary Etta Cobbet. They fell easily into the habit of lovingly and affectionately calling her Maryetta, a name that seemed more in keeping with her sunny and bright disposition.

Though the birth had been hard, the beauty and perfection of the little one softened June's heart considerably toward her husband and her plight. Though she was conscious of a creeping weariness and a loss of weight, she would never burden her family with complaint.

Ira had promised that before another year passed he would build them a new frame house with the river-rafted lumber that came from Wisconsin. He expected to sell some of his land-holdings in northern Iowa, and then they would move from their log-cabin penury and even hire help.

Lately everything about the two-room cabin seemed to irritate June and stir up resentment—the rough-hewn door, the three small windows that never let in enough air, the walls hung with bear skins and Mexican blankets. She even felt revulsion toward the furniture, for it brought back the days she had watched scorching suns and sudden rainstorms mar its beauty as it was being freighted to Iowa.

THE YOUNG DOCTOR HEADED his old, black-hooded Boston shay toward home, thinking about the little face that would be watching the road from the crudely carpentered window. Today was Maryetta's birthday, and with the natural expectancy of a five year old, she would be awaiting his return from his daily rounds. He had promised to bring her a very special surprise.

Maryetta had been born in the rude cabin six years after the territory had become a state. That had been in 1852, and she had never known the creature comforts of the East. For her there was no looking back on the blessings of another life.

Ira turned the wheels into the short graveled driveway and brought Molly, his horse, to a stop by the half shed. He'd hardly climbed down from the seat before he was accosted by a squealing Maryetta.

The child danced expectantly beside him as he walked toward the house, carrying a small black satchel in one hand and juggling a squirming brown sack in the other. She stood wide-eyed, patiently waiting as he deposited the sack in a large kettle that rested on the floor. Birthday or no, he wouldn't depart from his careful habit of scrubbing before embracing either a family member or supper. He performed the familiar ritual, lathering and scrubbing, and took a clean towel from Maryetta's hands.

"Don't keep her waiting any longer, Ira," said June. "She's not taken her eyes off the road since you left this morning!"

Merriment invaded the doctor's eyes, and he lifted Maryetta over his head and planted a bewhiskered kiss on her cheek.

"Why is that?" he asked, settling her back on the floor.

" 'Cause it's my birthday!" exclaimed Maryetta.

Ira scratched his head and feigned ignorance.

"Well, what do you know! How'd I manage to forget that?"

"You didn't forget, Papa. You're teasing! I know you have my present—and it's in that bag!"

"Well, bring the bag here and we'll have a peek!"

That was enough for Maryetta. Her quick hands were in the kettle and extricating the squirmy contents of the bag.

"It's alive!" she exclaimed, pulling a relieved kitten from the sack. "Oh, Papa, thank you. You kept your promise!"

Into his lap she climbed, with a choke-hold on the bewildered animal.

"What shall I name her?" she wondered aloud.

June had returned to the task of preparing the evening meal. She walked from hutch to stove, and back and forth from range to table, moving more slowly than usual.

"Folk coming into Davenport from Spirit Lake, putting up tents and lean-tos till they get their bearings," Ira announced. "Telling wild tales of the massacre there. Guess the Sioux really went on a rampage."

"Living's hard," June commented dully.

"Number of widows in the lot. My guess is they'll be heading back East in a matter of weeks."

June looked up from peeling potatoes.

"Word's about that Buchanan favors promoting the railroads. Don't know if Congress will back him—been too lackadaisical on the slavery issue. Won't settle well with the abolitionists," he continued.

June added wood to the fire and went to the hutch for dishes.

The sound of plates falling and splintering on the hard floor brought Ira Cobbet to his feet. Quickly depositing Maryetta and her kitten on the floor, he hurried to lift his unconscious wife. Her face ashen and her body limp, he carried her to their bedroom, placed her on the bed with her feet elevated, and reached for a bottle of ammonia. In a few moments color began to return to her face. She struggled to get up, but his hand restrained her.

"You are to remain in bed, June—and not for just a few hours—for several days."

Now the doctor was speaking, and it was clear he was alarmed. He looked at Maryetta's frightened expression.

"I'll get help in the morning," he said.

He was up early the following day and harnessing Molly. Maryetta watched him leave, setting off on the dusty road for town. Then she climbed onto her mother's bed for comfort.

"I will take care of you, Mama," she murmured.

"Of course you will, darling—I shall be better in no time."

Maryetta buried her face in her mother's gentle arms.

The doctor returned within an hour, bringing with him a short, plump, fair-complected woman.

"I have brought you help, June. This is Ellen MacDougal. She came in with the settlers from Spirit Lake. Says she can help for a few days—at least until the others head East. Says she won't mind sleeping in the loft with Maryetta."

Maryetta studied the woman closely. She had a nice face, all pink and white. Her eyes were a warm brown—like those of Esmerelda, their cow—and she spoke with a strong Scottish brogue. She gave the little girl a warm hug and set to work.

A week passed, and June Cobbet did not improve. When she

began to cough and run night fevers, Dr. Cobbet's fears were realized. He conferred with Ellen MacDougal more often. He also set to work hammering together a flimsy fence, which he then brought into the house.

Maryetta watched with dismay as he placed the strange contraption before her mother's open door and turned to her.

"You are not to go into your mother's room, Maryetta," he said soberly. "I have placed a barricade there just to remind you."

Maryetta was an obedient child. But how long would the fence be there? Was she never to be allowed near her mother? Would they ever again run in the tall grass together or sit together beside the fire and read? Would she feel the touch of Mama's lips on her forehead when she kissed her good night?

She lingered at the barrier, wistfully looking at the patient. Sometimes she brought small bouquets of columbine and wild roses, but only Ellen was allowed to take them to Mama.

Days moved on with the sound of Ellen bustling about with trays and basins—till one day, all the activity came to an abrupt halt. Whispering took the place of normal conversation, and an ominous dark presence moved in.

In hours, the wooden barrier was removed and Maryetta's father lifted her in his strong arms. They entered the forbidden room together. In an agony of grief and terror Maryetta looked down upon the quiet form of her mother and was told to say good-bye.

But this was not her mother! There was a stranger in Mama's bed. The hollow cheeks—the ghastly color—the sunken eyes.

"No, that's not mama—that's not my mama!" cried Maryetta. "I want my real mama—my pretty mama." Consumed with rage, the screaming child was carried from the room.

THE LOSS OF HIS wife sobered Ira Cobbet considerably, quenching his adventuresome and speculative spirit. He had not found it difficult to persuade Ellen MacDougal to stay on in her position of nursemaid and housekeeper; yet he began to have second thoughts about going on with this life in the wilderness. He felt the sting of guilt for not recognizing his wife's failing health. Perhaps he should return to New York so his small daughter would have a better life.

Eventually he began to sell off his land-holdings in the young state and make his traveling plans. It was not difficult to sell the land, for many Europeans as well as New Englanders and New Yorkers were emigrating to the West. In no time he had sold his assets at a profit and looked forward to purchasing a home in upstate New York once again.

"Will we take Tishme with us?" asked Maryetta.

The feline had earned its unusual appellation from the little girl's constant kisses and requests that the kitten kiss her back—only the order came out "Tish me," and the name had stuck.

"Yes, we will take Tishme," answered the doctor, eyeing the cat. She probably wouldn't survive the long trip.

"—and Ellen?"

"Of course—if she wants to come."

Thus it was that the foursome—Maryetta, Dr. Cobbet, Nurse Ellen, and Tishme—began the long trek back to New York. Foul weather and fair, ferry and stagecoach, long trails and dusty roads became the order of the day, until at long last they found themselves ascending broad front steps that led to a massive oaken door—a door that spelled the end to their long journey—a refuge where not only rest, but awesome beauty awaited them.

Maryetta turned questioning eyes toward her father.

"Is this where we are to live?" she asked uncertainly.

"This is home, Maryetta. Do you like it?"

"It's—it's—"

"I know. You will get used to it."

2

THE DOCTOR'S IMPRESSIVE NEW YORK HOME HAD, AT HIS bidding, been purchased and furnished for him by his sister. Miriam had outdone herself in an effort to quench forever his interest in the West; the scrolled-top desks on Chippendale frames, highboys on Cabriolet legs, ladder-back chairs, comb-back Windsors, and over stuffed winged chairs should keep him from ever again being tempted to invest in the uncertainties of the frontier.

Ellen's responsibilities were now just the kitchen and Maryetta. The doctor hired other servants to manage the rest of the large household.

For many days Maryetta and Tishme stepped off the thick, plush carpeting with distrust. The child looked forward more than ever to the assurances of her father when he came at evening from his busy-scheduled days. The sound of his returning chaise still held the magic of sweet reunion; she would curl up in his lap and fall asleep to the sound of his voice reading aloud to her. Time went mercifully on, assuaging the grief of the past.

For two years her Aunt Miriam's visits and solicitous efforts to plan social dinners for Papa brought an aura of enchantment to the big house. Maryetta found herself the unexpected center of attention at such functions, a small princess delighting in the favors and the compliments of her father's medical associates.

"How like she is to her beautiful mother." "How interesting

that she at least has the Cobbet eyes" . . . eyes as blue-gray as an August sky and framed with softly folded square lids. "How rewarding that she is so bright." The doctor must indeed be very proud of her!

Although always welcome at her father's dinner parties, what child could warm to the heavy topics discussed by his coterie of professional friends? A New Republican political party was in the making. The Kelly-Bessemer steel process was a monumental advancement in the science of iron processing. The establishment of a pharmaceutical association was under way. Maryetta found the company of Ellen and Tishme much more to her liking, and was content to observe her father's guests from the safety of an upstairs window.

Then Lydia Ashcroft appeared. The lady came upon the scene unobtrusively, as a guest of the doctor's closest friend. She had an aura of glamour, and her appearance both startled and attracted. Her height she accentuated by her custom of wearing feathers in her hair—but it was her eyes that first stirred Maryetta's apprehension. They were exceedingly blue, sharp, penetrating, and framed under the shortest of lids—as short and as cruel as a Tartar's, appraising while she pursued information from which she might gain.

She spoke in a youthful, animated way that drew attention. Her speech was direct, and her strange veneration for Europe's royal families was flagrantly reflected in her dress. She spoke often of her intention of being presented to England's queen. Her enthusiasm and her knowledge of current events engendered respect, particularly from the male guests.

The first time Maryetta met her face to face, the haughty guest, who had attached herself to the doctor's arm, turned to the child.

". . . and this is your little daughter, Ira! How quaint! We must find her more fitting attire than these Scotch plaids. You have a reputation to maintain, darling." She had scanned the well-chosen plaids Ellen had so carefully selected.

"But I like my dress!" Maryetta countered, cut to the quick.

The artful charmer laughed—a tinkling, sophisticated laugh—and tugged at the doctor's arm. "Poor dear, she has been without a mother much too long."

She walked Maryetta's father away, satisfied to have planted the seed of discontent, a seed that was quick to germinate and to have its influence in the days that followed.

As time went on, Maryetta noticed that Miss Ashcroft was coming to their house more and more often. Who was this woman who called her father "darling" and criticized her clothes? A new anxiety stirred within Maryetta.

More and more, Lydia began to make decisions for Ira Cobbet, most bordering on presumption. Dinner parties and guest lists came under her jurisdiction, and a discouraged Aunt Miriam felt her authority supplanted to the point that she gave up trying to help her brother.

On one of spring's first warm days, when the lilacs were sending their overwhelming fragrance into the air and their starlike lavender blossoms were enticing honeybees, the doctor walked his small daughter to the woods closely bordering the deep back lawn.

"Maryetta, as you grow older you will need a mother."

"I would like that," answered Maryetta enthusiastically.

She did not notice that her answer brought an expression of extreme satisfaction to her father's face.

"That is good, Maryetta, for I have asked Miss Ashcroft to be my wife."

Maryetta stopped walking and stood with her mouth open. If her father had struck her a blow, she could not have been more stunned. She burst into tears. Why, he had never even asked her what she thought of the woman! And wasn't Miss Ashcroft much younger than Papa? How could he marry her?

Yet there he stood expecting words of gratitude, and attributing her tears to relief and joy!

"There, there child. I had not intended to break it to you so suddenly."

He patted and cajoled, assuring her that now their lives would be complete.

The wedding plans moved ahead swiftly. Dr. Cobbet seemed vague and apart and in a sublime mood, and never once sensed his daughter's frustration.

With the nuptials performed and the honeymoon over, Lydia's complete domination of the doctor's affairs began. Servants who had been with the Cobbet household from the first days of their return from the West were given their dismissal and replaced by those of Lydia's preference. The doctor didn't seem to notice. To have someone in charge of the home seemed edelweiss to the busy physician, and when his wife's guest list began to include many of Europe's lesser royalty, he only prided himself on his wise selection of a helpmeet.

Thus it was that, under his approving eye, Lydia began her ambitious transformation of Maryetta. The house that had been Maryetta's to wander at will suddenly developed into territories, and the freedom she had always had to visit her father in the early morning and evening hours was suddenly removed.

"You must learn to curtsy!" said the autocratic newcomer one day.

"What is curtsy?" Maryetta asked innocently.

"A curtsy is a gesture of respect when one is in the presence of royalty—a nicely coordinated low bow."

"Oh. I thought cowboys were the only ones who did that—when they wanted a girl to dance with them."

The exasperated Lydia immediately went on a hunt for a dancing teacher, and to the chagrin of both teacher and pupil, opted to sit in on the miserable lessons.

"Why in the world your father could not have had a daughter with some semblance of refinement, I fail to understand. Maryetta, you can't or just won't act or think like a lady!"

The harsh criticism drove the child into a depressed state, turning her memory back to the wonderful days in Iowa and making her long for the gentleness of her own mother. She grew unusually quiet, appearing dull and even stupid to those who did not know her. Her one hope now was that her father's love and loyalty would in time free her from the dominance of her stepmother.

But even that hope began to fade, for with the passing of time, Lydia was succeeding in fastidiously claiming the doctor's every free moment for herself. Maryetta saw him less and less, till it seemed the only time she now spent with him was at the dinner hour.

It was at one such meal that the crowning blow came.

Lydia broached the subject in an offhand way—it was always with a casual air that she set her plans in action.

"Ira, dear, I have been thinking—I should like to take Maryetta to Europe."

"Europe?" queried the doctor, not guessing her intent.

"You may not have noticed, Ira, but Maryetta has all the earmarks of a frontier child. That is hardly conducive to a respectable future."

The doctor shifted uncomfortably in his chair.

"And what would you expect Europe to do for my daughter?" he asked.

"Early schooling does have its merits, dear."

Maryetta looked toward her father, whose face had changed color.

"But we have excellent schools right here," he protested, sending his daughter a reassuring smile.

"Not to be compared with Europe. You simply have no idea how well Europe's convents train their young ladies. Languages—Latin, French, German . . . Greek!"

"I rather prefer English, Lydia. I suggest we drop the subject."

It was the first time the doctor had opposed his new wife, and Maryetta saw the resentment smoldering in her hard eyes. Relieved as she felt by her father's reaction, she could see that it had only stirred up the abrasive nature of her stepmother. There would be storms ahead, of that she was certain.

"Why do you not support me? I am only trying to do something really fine for the child. I suppose you will find something wrong with my intention to be presented at England's court, too," Lydia declared. Miffed and flustered, she fled the table in a huff.

Maryetta and her father remained at the table, eating in silence and keenly aware that the peace of their lovely home had come to an end.

FOR DAYS AFTER THE encounter, quarreling was heard from the rooms of Dr. Cobbet and his wife. Lydia seemed to have little compunction about airing her quarrels before the servants—that was no doubt much of the art of gaining her way. Fragments of such quarrels came often to Maryetta's ears.

"—But Ira, you know that if that uncouth rail splitter is elected president, there will be a conflict!"

"I cannot see what that has to do with Maryetta."

"Well, I can. I shall be left with a child I hardly know, while you enlist for military duty!"

"Maryetta is a good child. She could scarcely be a problem—and you would always have Ellen."

"Ellen! With her miserable desecration of the King's English! Can't you see that I could never raise Maryetta without you?"

The planned alienation went on, with Lydia magnifying every childish antic into the grossest act of disobedience until Maryetta learned to avoid being in her presence as much as possible.

Toward the end of July the arguments had dissipated slightly, and Maryetta began to breathe easier.

August days came on with their usual humidity. One day dawned unmercifully hot with the prediction of ninety-eight degrees. The atmosphere of the house was steamy and sultry, and the gardens were languorous with only the droning of insects to disquiet the silence.

Tishme, though well past her kitten days, still showed an interest in the winged creatures that had multiplied with the coming of torrid weather. This day she had opted to settle in Maryetta's lap, where she purred contentedly and enjoyed the stroking of her mistress's small hands.

Suddenly a bee came in an opened window, and Tishme sprang from Maryetta's grasp. Jumping to her feet, she pursued the cat as it flew headlong toward the wide staircase. Maryetta scolded as she followed, explaining the severe consequences of interfering with the plans of a bee.

The door to her father's forbidden room was slightly ajar and Tishme, who cared little for rules or restrictions, dashed right in. Without thinking, Maryetta followed. She searched everywhere before spying a nervous twitching tail poking out from under the yellow skirt of the bed flounce. Springing with a celerity born of childish determination to end the silly chase, Maryetta managed to get hold of the protesting feline. With the cat in her arms she made a hasty retreat from the room—still scolding.

LYDIA WAS LATE THAT day returning from her dressmaker's. When she did arrive, she went straight to her room with her newly acquired finery. The doctor arrived home at his usual hour and sought out his wife's company.

Maryetta had not seen her stepmother since her arrival home. This was unusual; Lydia usually went about issuing orders before dinner. Then she saw her stepmother's private maid approaching.

"Your mother requests that you go to the library immediately," she said coldly.

Apprehensively Maryetta entered the library, where she saw her father sitting at his desk. Lydia stood behind him, a strange gleam in her narrowed eyes. Instinctively Maryetta knew she was in for something frightening, something momentous.

Her adversary had never looked more attractive; svelte in her new velvet suit, hair upswept and curls tight and smart over the crown of her head. She exuded confidence.

Something in her father's downcast eyes and silence told Maryetta that he had lost the battle with the clever woman.

Lydia spoke first. "Your behavior, Maryetta, is inexcusable. I have informed your father of your thievery!"

Maryetta's jaw sagged, and she looked from one to the other. "Thievery?" she asked.

"You cannot deny it, Maryetta. You were in my room, and you had been forbidden."

"I—I—was after—" She could not control her stammering.

"We know what you were after. My brooch is missing!"

Maryetta turned toward her father, her shock now merging and deepening with the flushed terror on her face. "Oh, Papa!" she breathed in unbelief.

But her father did not respond.

"Your bracelet was found under our bed. You cannot deny that you were there."

Once again Maryetta opened her mouth to explain, but Lydia cut in sharply to silence her.

"Your father and I are disappointed in you, and we have come to the conclusion that you need strong moral supervision. You and I shall be leaving for Europe in a matter of days, where you can expect to enter a convent school. Our decision is not to punish but to help you. We want you to see it that way."

Maryetta ran from the room and into the kitchen where Ellen was preparing dinner. She flung herself into the arms of her friend and burst into sobs.

Ellen rocked her gently until Maryetta could speak, patting and soothing as she had always done. Then she took Maryetta's face in her strong hands and kissed her.

"Now, lamb, can y'tell me?" she asked.

"Oh, Ellen, whatever will happen to me? She has lied about me, and Papa believes her. He never said one word. Oh, Ellen, he believes I am a thief—and I am to be sent away. Why, Ellen—why?"

"There, there. We'll get to the bottom of this. Don't you fret."

But Ellen, too, was shocked and dared not show her disapproval nor her distrust lest she burden Maryetta more.

The plans were made swiftly—surely with Lydia engineering the entire plot. Speedily the suitcases were packed, and the day of their departure drew near.

Maryetta's father called her to his office, on his face a look of humility and in his voice a tinge of shame.

"You will be going to Belgium, Maryetta, but it will not be for long. That I can assure you. There is certain to be a war here in this nation, and I shall be obliged to offer my services and skills to the Union. I would not be here to see to your good. Do you understand?"

Maryetta buried her chin in the ruffles of her dress.

"I shall come for you as soon as possible. The South has limited means for waging a successful war—it cannot last for very long. So be a brave little girl."

Maryetta struggled to hold back the tears, but it was a futile effort. They rolled down her cheeks and into her mouth.

Later, Lydia came to Maryetta's room in a deceitfully conciliatory mood.

"I know how difficult it has been for you to call me mother," she began, "but that will soon change. When I have been presented to England's Queen I expect to be addressed as 'Madame Cobbet.' That should please you."

EVENTS WERE MOVING SO fast that Maryetta found herself caught in an ennui of despondency and dull fear. Knowing nothing of deceit and retaliation, she moved from day to day awaiting the unknown and wearing the expression of a hunted animal. Her tears had run their solitary course, and Maryetta secretly vowed that she would never again give the cruel Lydia the satisfaction of seeing her cry.

"We leave in the morning, Maryetta, so I expect you to be up early," said Lydia in as officious a tone as ever. "Your father and Ellen will see us off."

As they took the trains to the shipyards and boarded the docked liner, Maryetta's heart felt like lead. She kissed her father and Ellen good-bye, ascended the gang plank, and hurried to the railing to wave. She stood there in a thoroughly resigned state of mind. If her father expected obedience, then she would do her best to meet his expectations, though she could not understand his reasoning.

But as the great vessel began to move away from its moorings, and the distance between her and those she loved most dearly began to widen, Maryetta was seized with such overwhelming terror that she forgot her resolve.

"No, no! I don't want to go! Oh, please—someone stop this boat!"

The words broke from her lips and she wrestled herself free from Lydia's restraining hands. Running down the deck toward the stern, she made a clumsy attempt to climb the rail. As she was about to plunge into the swirling waters, she felt strong hands coming down upon her shoulders. A deck steward dragged her away protesting and weeping, and she was rudely carried and locked in her stateroom. Now she was really a prisoner of her hated stepmother.

Undaunted, she pushed a chair to a porthole and looked out upon the oily, rushing waters. They were in the channel and rapidly moving toward the sea.

Swept with the knowledge of her loss, overcome with hatred for Lydia, eight-year-old Maryetta made a solemn vow. Never would she rest until she had repaid that evil woman for her treachery. Never would she give up her purpose—to someday have her revenge!

3

MARYETTA SPENT THE FIRST DAYS ON THE ROLLING SEAS IN THE close atmosphere of a stateroom steadfastly refusing to eat. A sympathetic steward brought food to her; by the end of the fourth day his kindness convinced her to take some nourishment, but the girl cared little whether she survived.

Lydia, so enraptured with her own plans, seemed not to notice.

Several times in the nineteen days of ocean travel, squall clouds came in overhead, followed by rain and high seas that hindered the progress of the screw-propeller steamship. Just as Maryetta had grown used to the heaving and rolling of the vessel, word came that they were in sight of the shores of Britain. Conversation with her stepmother had deteriorated to short, clipped sentences interspersed with threats that her father would be informed if she did not cooperate.

Maryetta was young, but not so young that she could not realize she was being held in an evil, paralyzing web. By the time they docked in Southampton, she had so withdrawn that she did not speak at all. She went silently along with her complaining parent as Lydia sought to hire a carriage for London, not even noticing the hunted animal look that was again stamping the child's features.

They stayed for many days in London. Maryetta was shunted off into the care of older women with strange sounding accents and voracious appetites for gossip. Lydia, meanwhile, preened for her scheduled presentation at court and gathered with women of like purpose. Their conversations were full of the lives of Europe's royal families; their engagements, their children, the Austrian Elizabeth's travels, Britain's Princess Royal and her Prussian Prince.

A few times Maryetta heard men discussing the possibility of a war in the United States and what that would do for British shipping, but with no family anchor, neither future nor friend, she continued to build a wall around herself and close out communication with everyone.

Mercifully for Maryetta, the London stay finally came to an end. Lydia had to resign herself to the environs of common folk. She was off to an inn and making plans to go to Dover and ultimately to the European Continent.

"You will dress warmly, Maryetta. It can be windy and damp in the channel, and the trip will take several hours. I don't intend for you to arrive with a cold. You must be at your best for our interview."

But Maryetta was already feeling ill. Her head ached and her throat hurt, and the odors from the ferry did little to alleviate her suffering.

Within five hours after embarking, the high-reeded embankments that protected the Belgium port of Oostende came into view. From Oostende they took a coach to a train station and were rapidly passing South of Ghent and Aalst. Here Maryetta got her first view of the verdant hills and flagrant colors of well-kept gardens as well as the austerity of textile buildings and grain storehouses.

So this was Belgium! This was a new place for the bewildered Maryetta. It was not the great plains of young America, nor the growing metropolis of New York, but a new place to wonder about—perhaps to fear—a place called Belgium!

For the first time since leaving New York, Maryetta's interest was piqued. The landscape was so very different from anything she had ever seen. The strange little country had much to offer: the rivers Leie and Schelde, canals, towering church steeples, the

Belfry of St. Barvos. Then they entered the outskirts of Brussels.

Belgium was a place as diversified as the North and South of the United States, its history chronicled in its architecture, statuary, and battlefields; from the early Belgae tribes to the Merovingian kings, from the good reign of Charlemagne to the ambitious onslaught of Napoleon's armies, from kings, dukes, prince bishops and counts to the ochlocracy of the Flemings and Walloons—a country of distinct character.

Its situation on the northeast European coast had made the little country a veritable chessboard, and it had suffered and invited multiple invasions and dominance from all directions. Prudently its people had accepted the changing winds of government as their own peculiar lot, learning well to compromise with their enemies in order to retain the dignity of being a nation among nations.

By 1831 the German Prince of Saxe-Coburg Saalfeld had become Belgium's King Leopold I, but Maryetta knew nothing of this as she was hurried along by the carping, disagreeable Lydia.

"Walk faster, Maryetta, or we shall be late for our appointment!"

"Oh, Madame . . . please . . . I am so tired . . . and it is hot!"

But Lydia did not slacken her pace. Instead she gave the child a yank and continued with her chiding and impatience.

"Why must you complain so? And don't fidget with your hat—you may not take it off. Catholics wear hats, and we must make a favorable impression."

"I'll take if off when we get there—and my shoes and my coat!"

"You will be on your best behavior or I shall tell your father," warned the resolute woman, looking around for a carriage to hire.

An astute coachman, whose living depended on his felicity and good English, was quick to see the baffled American and drive his carriage to the curb.

"Where to, Madame?" he asked with surprisingly fair English and inflated pride. With polite solicitation he took off his hat and bowed.

Lydia placed a piece of paper in his hands. With a nod he

helped the two into his vehicle, cracked a whip smartly, and headed off into the recently built Boulevard Ring.

Almost immediately they were in the bustle of the Grand Place where Maryetta could see, just beyond the wide brim of her hat, the towering, magnificent guild houses. See, too, the shining figure of St. Michael brazenly crushing Lucifer beneath his feet.

"Why do the buildings seem to grow right out of the sidewalks?" she asked.

"Hush!" came the answer.

Still straining to see to the top of the guild houses, Maryetta noticed that they were climbing a slight rise and entering what seemed to be the private sector. Houses were multi-gabled with finely crafted wrought iron fencing, the architecture *fin de siecle*. Little shrines were carved right into the walls of the dwellings.

The coach came to an abrupt halt before a large stone edifice. They descended to fanning flagstones that led to the front door where they entered a glassed-in vestibule. With a mixture of childish curiosity and apprehension, Maryetta appraised her strange surroundings while Lydia pulled on a bell.

The two stood waiting while the heat of the enclosure stirred a warning of nausea in Maryetta's stomach. She could hear the sound of the bell reverberating through the interior and wondered if the door would ever open.

Suddenly a middle-aged woman in nun's habit stood before them, an inscrutable expression on her dark features.

"I am Madame Cobbet," said Lydia, wearing the title as ostentatiously as she wore the speckled pheasant plumage of her hat.

"*Entrez vous*," said the doorkeeper, apparently not impressed by her American guests.

They fell in behind the nun and walked quietly down the corridors, which boasted artistically carved doors, each clearly numbered. They entered an office where the ceilings were cathedral high. One tall window reached nearly to the ceiling and was without curtain or drape. A desk, three chairs, and a long, low wooden bench were all that furnished the room and, except for the opening and closing of doors, it was extremely restful—cool and quiet. In a hollowed-out shrine on one wall was a sculptured figure of the Deipara.

Papa would take a fit if he could see me here! thought Maryetta ruefully. *Even worse—if he could know how sick I feel!*

"S'il vous plait, asseyez vous," said the young nun, pointing to a chair.

That was easy to understand, and Maryetta struggled up onto a large chair while Lydia seated herself stiffly in another.

They were not there long before they heard the rustle of a heavy woolen skirt, and a woman past middle-age appeared. She too was clad in the habit of the order, with wide pleats on the bodice and a ropelike tie at her waist. She was round-faced in a pleasant sort of way with cheeks scrubbed and ruddy. Her teeth were polished, giving her broad smile an impressive shining brightness. She moved with natural competency, exuding efficiency. There was little doubt that she was the one in charge of the convent's affairs.

"Good afternoon, Mrs. Cobbet," she said in English, with only a trace of an accent. "We have been expecting you. Mercy! The child looks miserable. Do remove your coat, child!"

She lifted a small brass bell from her desk and shook it. Immediately the nun who had opened the front door returned.

"Get this poor child a drink of water, Sister, and help her off with her hat and coat."

Her tone was magistrative, having also an element of sympathy, and the nun did as she was directed.

"Please—my shoes, too," begged the flushed Maryetta.

Removing the shoes, the nun turned brusquely toward her superior.

"L'enfant a très chaud. Est-elle malade?"

Noticing Lydia's blank expression, the prioress translated. "She says the child is running a fever. Is she ill?"

"She was not ill when we arrived in Oostende," said Lydia.

"Sister Josephine, please take her to her room and see that she rests. No doubt the journey has been long for one so young."

"I have seen no sign of illness!" protested Lydia.

The older woman ignored the denial and rummaged through a stack of papers.

As Maryetta left, she heard Lydia's voice trailing after her. It sickened her more to realize her stepmother would lie to a woman of the church . . . but she was much too ill to care.

"YOU SAY HER NAME IS MARIE?"

"She is called Maryetta."

"We shall call her 'Marie.' "

"As you wish," said Lydia with a shrug. "But she won't take readily to the change. Perhaps in time. . . ."

"Now! You will want a quarterly report?"

"Yes."

"And letters, of course, when she learns to write legibly."

"That will not be necessary."

The Prioress, her eyes narrowed and thoughtful, studied Lydia.

"Sister Josephine will take you to your daughter's room to say good-bye," she said.

"Do you mind? I should prefer to spare her."

"As you wish."

Lydia made a hurried curtsy and left.

SICK AND FRIGHTENED, MARYETTA clung tenaciously to the hand of the woman leading her. Her head was spinning, her body aching and heavy. Once she pulled back.

"*Allez—Allez!*" prodded the nun.

Maryetta looked weakly at the woman.

"*Allez—Marie!*" she repeated.

"My name is not Marie! I am Maryetta!"

But her protest was ignored, for it was clear that Sister Josephine knew little if any English. The nun opened a numbered door, and they stepped inside a long, large room. Seven cots lined the longest side of the room. Opposite the beds, arranged neatly so that they touched, were separate washstand commodes, each topped with a small pitcher in a round porcelain bowl.

Sunshine poured in from a casement of windows at the far end of the room. The Sister opened a closet door and hung Maryetta's hat and coat on a low hook, then returned with a hairbrush and smoothed the damp curls from Maryetta's forehead. She indicated that Maryetta was to lie down on one of the narrow beds, which the child was only too willing to do. Sister Josephine covered her with a light gray blanket.

"Am I to live here?" asked Maryetta, lips quivering and tears ready to flow.

Sister Josephine looked puzzled, shook her head, and left the room, leaving Maryetta to wonder if she had said no or simply did not understand.

Alone, Maryetta could still feel the motion of the ferry and smell the oil and the brine of the sea. Feeling sick and abandoned, she closed her eyes, hoping that would shut out the unfamiliar, pungent odor of boxwood. It was not long before she had drifted off into the mercy of exhausted sleep.

When she awoke, she could see the flickering light of the candles that lined the walls. They were set in wall sconces designed with metal fleurs-de-lis. She lay very still, fearing what would come next.

Suddenly the door opened and a group of young girls entered, all in orderly fashion. They spoke in subdued tones in a foreign language. Quickly they were at the basins and preparing for bed. Clasping rosary beads they knelt, prayed, and then climbed under the gray blankets.

Maryetta swallowed hard and flung her own blanket over her head.

"No—no—no, Marie!"

It was a new voice and a new face. A nun was uncovering her head and holding a cup to Maryetta's lips. The liquid tasted sweet, like the niter Maryetta's own father had administered in the past, and the memory brought on a flood of tears. The Sister patted the tears away, making kind, sympathetic little noises, and then she was gone. Through the night she came twice, and by the morning the fever had left.

Maryetta arose in the early gray of dawn and crept toward the windows. Looking down upon the cobblestones, she shivered. The Belgian street was now mackerel mottled from the wind-blown tree shadows. What could possibly be ahead? To whom could she speak? And Lydia—where had she gone? Not that she expected any kindness from her stepmother, but at least there had been the possibility of communication.

A jangling, earsplitting bell sounded, interrupting Maryetta's thoughts. The obstreperous urgency of the sound sent a wave of panic through her small frame. Should she run or stand still?

The oldest girl of the group arose sleepily from her bed and stood facing the terrified apparition by the window.

"*Qui êtes-vous?*" the girl asked uncertainly.

Maryetta gulped. It was obviously a question. How might she answer?

Mercifully, a nun entered the room and began issuing sharp commands. Whatever she said, it seemed to bring order out of chaos and to direct each child to her own commode. Now, instead of blatant gawking, the children only stole quick glances in Maryetta's direction.

Touching Maryetta's forehead, the nun gave her a warm smile of relief and proceeded to fill a basin with water for her. Next she reached for a brush and vigorously applied it to Maryetta's tangled curls. Pulling so hard that it brought the sting of tears to Maryetta's eyes, she tied the girl's hair at the back.

"No, no. I do not wear my hair so!"

But the nun seemed deaf to Maryetta's protests. Maryetta

noticed that with the exception of one girl, whose taffy-colored hair was braided and wrapped around her head, all of the others had their hair in the same style.

The nun clapped her hands for attention, and the children came toward her, stretching small arms into little brown jackets.

"*Je m'appelle Soeur Agnes,*" she explained, pointing to herself and repeating the name.

She then called each child separately to her side and began introductions.

"Antoinette, Clarice, Louise, Charlotte, Florence, Janine, and Isobel." She pointed to Maryetta and mouthed a name that sounded like "Marie Corbay."

Maryetta felt keen disappointment. How would she know when they were speaking to her? How would they ever know her real name? This Corbay name was not hers.

"Please, good lady, I am Maryetta Cobbet. Do not call me by that other name."

Sister Agnes looked perplexed, as did the children, and the nun turned to dismiss the group.

Maryetta, however, was grasped by the hand and led to a large dining hall. There must have been at least fifty girls there, ranging in ages from six to sixteen, and all in identical brown suits.

Maryetta recognized the broad-faced prioress immediately. She was seated at the head table and smiling pleasantly. Sister Agnes led her charge up to the big table, where the prioress took Maryetta's small hand in her warm plump one and with the other reached for a small brass bell. Maryetta wondered if the kind-looking woman spent her life ringing bells.

Then she spoke in English—music to Maryetta's ears—and Maryetta warmed toward the woman instantly.

"Marie Corbay, we welcome you. May the saints bless you as you join us and may you adjust well to our family and our ways." She then reverted back to her French and addressed the roomful of girls.

With her eyes riveted to the floor, Maryetta felt afresh the abandonment of all human caring. Her thoughts were interrupted by the sound of the girls singing, and since they were all looking at her, she could only assume that she was hearing a traditional welcoming song.

Back to the breakfast she went with her own age group. Sister Agnes poured a generous glassful of milk for her and encouraged her to eat. Surprisingly, the table fare was remarkably varied. The small country had a reputation for supplying her citizenry with plenty, and here before Maryetta's eyes was ample proof of their boast.

The opening of school was still evidently weeks away, but for the students there was an orientation period. Maryetta wondered what would follow. After breakfast she went with her group to a small church close to the convent. She watched as each child knelt to offer her prayers. High on the wall at the front of the building was an enormous hand-carved wooden cross with the figure of the Christ stretched upon it.

The cruel wooden sculpture made Maryetta wince. She had heard something of the historic and gentle Jesus in the small white church in Iowa with her father. That had been in the weeks following her mother's death—now it seemed very long ago. Had He too lived in a world of heartless people? Who could have nailed Him to those wooden beams? She wondered secretly if Jesus had ever managed to get off the cross—ever succeeded in freeing Himself from the agony imposed upon Him by a world of selfish people. Most surely He, too, had been lied about and destined to suffer!

Returning to the convent, Maryetta was given her own paints and introduced for the first time to projects that stirred her interest. Most impressive was the room full of older girls who worked silently and diligently on the most exquisite writing Maryetta had ever seen.

By evening, the little narrow cot in the long room looked more welcome than she could ever have dreamed possible, and she got into bed exhausted. She would have fallen asleep instantly if it had not been for a strange sensation that someone was standing by her bed.

She opened her eyes and looked into the face of a young girl her own age smiling down at her. At first Maryetta wondered if it were possible that one of the cherubs she had seen on the chapel's frescoed wall might have come to life and followed her back to the convent. But the pretty girl reached out and touched Maryetta's face, and the gesture touched a responding chord in her lonely heart. She smiled back, wishing there might be a universal language, one everyone could comprehend.

Maryetta was much too young to realize that they had exchanged a message in the only language that was universal. She knew only that the touch and the smile of Janine Turgot had eased the pain in her own heart.

The following day Maryetta was taken to a sewing class where she watched the young ladies at work, each with her own project. An older girl showed Maryetta how she laid patterns on the brown cloth and cut them out. She indicated that one of the uniforms they were cutting would soon be Maryetta's.

The days were so busy that Maryetta had little time to dwell on her plight. She began quietly and with interest to study the older girls as well as her peers. It seemed that some of the older girls were frequently assigned to the younger children's rooms as a kind of resident monitor, to teach the little ones the routine of the convent. They were pleasant girls and related well to the little newcomers.

Of course the children her own age attracted her most, and she yearned to know them as friends.

Sandy-haired Antoinette seemed to have come from the aristocracy, for she received more gifts and more mail than the others. Her most treasured gift, in this building that seemed to be without mirrors, was a jeweled hand mirror which she shared, but sparingly.

Clarice was of the bourgeoisie, a likable person who did her work well and minded her own business. Her features were distinctly Walloon and not very regular, but her affable nature shone through.

Charlotte and Isobel seemed to be bosom pals, possibly from the same city, for they were inseparable, sharing childish secrets to the exclusion of the others.

Louise was a round-faced, fair-complected child with extremely sad, large blue eyes. That, with the ash-blonde hair braided and wrapped around her head, gave her a Tyrolean appearance. Later Maryetta learned that Louise had recently been orphaned, which explained why she cried so frequently.

Janine, the little ambassador who had reached out to Maryetta on the American girl's second night at the school, was the one to whom Maryetta gravitated. She was definitely the friendliest, with lovable winning ways and a jolly sense of humor. She could spread a special kind of sunshine to the bleakest of situations. In the evenings she mimicked the dignified nuns by throwing a towel over her head and tripping purposely on her long, gray nightgown. When she wasn't playacting, she was testing her skill at jumping from bed to bed without falling, wincing with pain and grinning gamely. Everyone seemed to love Janine—with the exception of Florence.

Florence was a girl of somber expression who seldom joined the others in their moments of revelry. She gave Maryetta a feeling of distrust, for one could rarely guess what went on behind the inflexible features.

It seemed that no one had jewelry, so it surprised Maryetta that a number of the older girls had gold watches. There was a distinct conformity of clothing and privilege here, so she wondered how a few had come by the lovely jewelry.

BY THE BEGINNING of the school year, Maryetta could understand a little of the new language. Though she could speak yet but poorly, she understood a few oft repeated phrases.

Chapter Three

As Christmas drew near, she was delighted to discover that there was a definite change of pace, a relaxing of heavy schedules and stiff regulations. The days of pageantry and processions took the edge off her loneliness and gave her an opportunity to take a fresh look at her peers. If she were to survive in this new world, she would need the goodwill and support of at least a few of her roommates.

She was certain she could never trust Florence. Instinctively she sensed that any effort to make friends with her would be repulsed. Isobel and Charlotte had made it clear that theirs was an impenetrable clique and no intruder would be welcome. That left three others—and the miserable hindrance of a foreign language!

Janine was everyone's friend. Her affable disposition could engender neither rivalry nor resentment. She presented no problem.

Antoinette was the one who studied her. Maryetta often looked up from her studies to find the girl gazing at her. Several times she had left her own studies and stood at Maryetta's shoulder. It had frightened Maryetta until Antoinette reached with her pen and corrected the American girl's work. Gratitude welled up inside her at the unexpected kindness, and a wall was broken down. The incident soon developed into a game, and sometimes the other friendly ones joined in.

Last was Louise—the left-out one, the sad-eyed, bereaved child with the angelic face. This was one Maryetta must help; she must convey to her love and sympathy, and let the girl know that she, too, had experienced losses.

At breakfast one morning, the Reverend Mother announced that there were special holiday events the girls could anticipate. One was the presentation of their annual Christmas play. Of course, Maryetta's inability to speak French eliminated her from having a part, but there were others also content to be part of the audience.

When the evening arrived, excitement filled the air with magic. The girls made their way single file into the large dining room, where tables had been cleared away and decorations and a crude curtain hung.

Maryetta waited breathlessly for the first act to begin. In spite of her language limitations, she was quick to grasp the humorous plot as it unwound. It seemed that the work of St. Nicholas was being constantly hampered by a mischievous imp—none other than Janine Turgot!

Who could be more suited to the role? She danced about, grimaced and cavorted with abandonment, bringing giggling approval from her audience. The heaviness of school-day schedules was forgotten, and the children were swept into the cheer of the season.

Louise was scheduled to appear in the second act. Maryetta could hardly wait to see her, for she had been given the coveted role of a departed saint. Louise came on the platform hesitantly, her lovely long ashen hair flowing . . . and her wide blue eyes terrified. She looked out at the audience, opened her mouth to speak—and fainted! The play came to an unexpected end as a group of nuns hastily carried Louise off.

The girls were allowed to visit their recovering classmate and convey their sympathies. Maryetta saw her opportunity and hurried to her room to draw a picture for Louise. She drew two stick figures on a page; one had a mop of curly blonde hair and the other had long flowing hair. There was no question whom they represented. The hand clasp of the two figures was grossly enlarged.

When it was Maryetta's turn to offer condolences, she presented her artwork, pointed to the figures and then to Louise and herself. Louise understood immediately, and a smile spread over her face. She reached for Maryetta and planted a kiss on her cheek. The door of communication had been opened, and for days afterward the two girls sent drawings back and forth. Maryetta had won a friend.

ONCE A PRETTY POSTCARD came in the mail from Aunt Miriam, bringing a rare smile to Maryetta's face. There came also news that a man by the name of Abraham Lincoln had been elected her nation's sixteenth president. He would assume his office in January, and the sure likelihood of a war was discussed by the Sisters.

Such discussions brought back to Maryetta the solemn prediction her father had made and the possibility that he would offer his services to the Union. Would he forget his promise to her? Had he missed her as much as she had missed him? And why, oh, why had he neglected to write—was she always to go on wondering what was happening at the big brick house?

In the midst of all her questions, a package arrived for Maryetta. Her faithful old nurse had sent it, with a note explaining that she could not forget her dear child with Christmas so near. The package contained a well-done likeness of Maryetta's father in his uniform, painted on ivory. It brought hot tears to her eyes, but also unexpected joy, for now she could display her treasures to her peers. No one would guess that she had been abandoned.

With the holidays behind her, Maryetta began to settle into the convent routine. Art class became her favorite time, for there she could enter into the wonderful world of color and lines and find a measure of peace in accomplishment.

But she frequently wondered what the new year would bring.

4

SO WELL DIRECTED AND DISCIPLINED WAS THE SCHOOL YEAR THAT followed that it left few idle moments for Maryetta to dwell upon her strange exile. The orientation to so much that was foreign and new also kept her thoughts from wandering to the injustices of the past.

At age nine she found herself with a cool outward indifference facing a second Christmas in the land of religious processions, street carolers, and solemn observances. She was both mystified by and impressed with the reverence the Belgians displayed toward their ecclesiastical heritage and their royal family. They seemed to have a rare appreciation for their adored regents.

The feeling was apparently mutual, for it was not uncommon for the much-loved Leopold and his queen to be seen riding through the streets, waving cordially to bystanders. Often, too, much ado was made about a visit from England's royal family. So when news came on December 14 that Victoria's beloved Albert had succumbed to the dreaded typhoid, the period of mourning that followed robbed the season of its expected joy. But Maryetta had become stoically conditioned to the fact that death was as much a part of life as birth.

By Christmas Eve restrictions were somewhat relaxed, and the convent children were allowed to march through the streets to the Church of Notre Dame du Sablon, passing Saint Hubert's statue with his many-tined stag, caroling the oft repeated ancient songs of God's holy gift to the world. The children were treated to a glimpse of the crèche at the altar, and stood sucking their fingers and wondering at the Incarnation and what it all had to do with them. They were then guided quietly back to the convent.

Christmas dinner was made up of rare treats, beginning with *waterzooi,* not made with fish this time, but with fowl. *Witloof poele* was also served, and little *boudin blanc* morsels in applesauce. For dessert, each child received a small cut of *couques de dinant* and a miniature painted card of the angel Gabriel announcing his divine message to Mary.

It was a drastic departure from the rigid and tedious schedule, and Maryetta was not without gratitude for the respite. She held the gingerbread and the card so tightly in her fist that the two homogenized into a sticky brown mass. Nevertheless, it was her own treasured possession and more so, since once again, with the exception of Aunt Miriam's card, there had been neither remembrance nor Christmas greeting from home.

Sister Agnes, who had been observing Maryetta, did her best to help the child forget her disappointment by taking her outside to a small pond that had frozen overnight. For a brief time Maryetta watched the good sister fall repeatedly, her high black shoes slipping precariously on the treacherous ice, her veil and her dignity tossed to the winds. She shrieked and laughed, hoping to draw Maryetta into the fun, but after only a short time Maryetta retreated to the sidelines, thanking Sister Agnes for her kindness. She still had to face the other children. What would she say when they asked to see her gifts?

When twilight began to move in, Maryetta managed to slip away unnoticed. In the excitement of the day she was sure she would not be missed. With the gingerbread still crushed in her fist, she sought her own bed and climbed under the covers.

Back home, aunts and uncles would be arriving at the big brick house. If she were there, she'd be listening to the bells on the sleighs, hearing them long before they came into view. The guests would be arriving laden with brightly trimmed packages, and some already would have found their places at the piano. Music and laughter would be filling the house and she herself would be in the kitchen watching as Ellen basted the savory geese. Maryetta pulled the covers over her head and sobbed.

The door opened and Maryetta pretended to be sleep. She heard someone cross the room and look in upon her. A small hand went under her pillow, and then the visitor was gone. Wonderingly, Maryetta reached under her pillow and felt a small bottle. She withdrew the unexpected gift and looked at it. It was the same gift of toilet water Janine had received from her family.

The gesture brought on fresh tears, tears that only made Maryetta angry, for never must her peers discover the turmoil that went on inside of her. Frustrated and spent, she again pulled the covers over her head and drifted off to sleep.

She awoke with a start when she heard the rustle of heavy garments. No doubt it was Sister Anunciata come to force her to join the others. She would be taken to the big dining hall and have to explain why there had been no gifts from home. The humiliation would be unbearable!

Peering through a small aperture in her blanket sanctuary, Maryetta could see a nun lighting the wall candles. Then she went to each commode and placed a small red candle at each.

It was a sister Maryetta had never seen before. The tiny golden flames sent yellow warmth over the stranger's face, and for a moment Maryetta thought perhaps she had died and gone to heaven. The stranger must be an angel! Her features were so calm—so fine and so beautiful—her smile so gentle—her skin all white and cheeks soft and pale pink.

The nun stood looking at the wide-eyed child. "Marie Corbay?"

It was only a whisper, but the gentle voice made the hated name sound beautiful.

Maryetta responded as she had been taught. *"Oui, Soeur."*

"Maryetta—why are you not with the others?"

The lovely vision had spoken in English and used her own

name! Now Maryetta was more than certain she had died.

"You are lonely," said the nun, answering her own question and observing the tear-stained face.

"Yes, Sister—but I do not know you. Who are you?"

The nun walked to Maryetta's bed and sat down, taking Maryetta's small hand in her own with the warm touch of a mother.

"I am new here. I have come from Mechelen."

"How are you called?"

"I am Sister Celeste. But come, you must not be alone on Christmas!" She began to remove the covers and to pull Maryetta to her feet.

"Oh, please, Sister, do not make me join the others—please!"

"I have no such intention, little one. Come!"

Together they walked into the corridor and on into several more until the Sister stopped at one of the strange concave doors Maryetta had often wondered about. They entered a small, compact cell and closed the door behind them.

The furnishings were of simple design, consisting only of the most necessary pieces: a bed, a chair, a bureau, a table, and a metal brazier. The bright angel then proceeded to light a small candle and place it on the table. Speedily then she was at the brazier and blowing into the gray coals until they started up red.

"We shall have our Christmas supper together, Maryetta. I have paine à la greque and tea—and time away from duties. Here! Cut us some bread!" She handed Maryetta a small ivory-handled knife.

"Did you say it is Greek bread?" asked Maryetta.

"*Oui!* Strangely, bread of which the Greeks have never heard. It had its origin in one of the Augustinian monasteries!"

She laughed a wonderfully joyous laugh, transforming the dark little cell into a splendid castle, filling even the corners with sunshine and reaching into Maryetta's heart.

"You speak English." It was a statement filled with wonder.

"I have been trained. That is why I am here. Perhaps you have noticed—more children are coming from America. I have been sent to train for the position of duenna for them. In a way I must prove myself before being blessed with the title. Come, let us make tea. You do drink tea?"

The nun had taken a tiny kettle from off the coals and was already pouring the scalding water into a little teapot.

"And put jam on your bread!" she ordered.

Maryetta complied, recalling the many times she had sat with Ellen in the big kitchen.

"Tell me, little one, what gifts have you received?"

Instantly the charm of the tryst was broken. Maryetta looked down and bit her lip in an effort to keep it from quivering.

"Aah—I see. Perhaps your gifts have been delayed in transit. That does happen, you know. But come, tell me—if you were to wish for something special—that is, if you had one wish, what would it be?"

"I do not dare to wish, Sister."

"Nonsense. Make a wish!"

Maryetta considered. If this new friend were playing a game, she would go along.

"I guess—I'd wish this dreadfully tight band on my hair could be removed. Just once I'd like to wear my hair the way my mother and Ellen used to fix it."

"Who is Ellen?"

"Ellen was my nurse—my dear, wonderful nurse. She used to dip a comb in hot water and make curls around her fingers."

"That should not be difficult—if you would not mind using the last of your tea. The fire has died down, and I am allotted only so many coals."

She went to the commode and retrieved a large comb from a drawer.

"You are going to curl my hair?"

"Of course, but it must remain our secret. You may have observed that vanity is likely to be frowned upon here."

It was sheer pleasure to feel Sister Celeste's capable fingers rolling her hair into curls and to enjoy the sparkling conversation. But all too soon it was time for the visit to end.

"I am not allowed to show preference, Maryetta, so I must call you Marie as the prioress has directed. Will you understand that?"

Maryetta nodded.

"And of course we shall keep our secret about this tête a tête. You know the way back to your room, *n'est-ce pas?*"

Maryetta nodded again and left with eyes shining and heart singing.

Her peers came in later, filing past the sleeping American girl and wondering how she could have curled her hair so beautifully—and why she was smiling in her sleep.

5

THE MEMORY OF THAT WONDERFUL CHRISTMAS WHEN GOD HAD sent an angel in the person of Sister Celeste remained, the savoring of it sweet and comforting to Maryetta's bruised heart, and another long year came to an end.

By the time the summer of 1863 had turned into fall and her fourth school year in Belgium had begun, Maryetta had learned to speak simple sentences in French and to communicate with her peers. Except for Aunt Miriam's annual Christmas card with its apologies for her brother's silence, there was no word from home.

The convent routine was so stringent that Maryetta had little time to nurse her wounds and less to send out letters. She gave up hoping to stir her father into action. But there were times when memories swept in upon her and she felt his unkind disregard and lack of compassion. Only the sweet encouragement of Celeste kept Maryetta from giving up hope altogether.

The winter was a good one and passed well enough with Maryetta improving in many skills. Throughout the summer, Celeste took her on many tours of Brussels, until she began to feel part of the city that had so bewildered her at first.

By 1864 there was a filtering in of war news from the States, but it was seldom given first place in the European theater. Maryetta, nearly twelve years old, had changed outwardly. Gone was the baby-faced child and in her place an awkward, unsure adolescent.

Sister Celeste had proven herself and was now very much in charge of the American students, but never once did she neglect her first charge. She worked tirelessly to help her gain confidence and trust in herself and adjust to her confined life.

One day the Sister suggested that they explore the convent building. The suggestion piqued Maryetta's adolescent curiosity, but more, the consideration from the kind woman was something the girl craved. Together they walked the many corridors, descended basement stairs, and explored many rooms. Most were used for storage; here a book-room, there food supplies, here medical supplies, there valued writing materials—all neatly stacked and labeled.

Then they climbed a dark, narrow staircase that led to the garret rooms. The door at the top of the stairs opened into a large sunny room with attractive casement windows. A good number of braziers burned brightly, dispelling the dampness of early spring and softening the austerity of simple furnishings. Women sat in a circle, their heads bent over lap boards, engrossed in some sort of handwork.

At first Maryetta was aware only that the seated occupants were nuns wearing the conventional habit of the order. A closer observation revealed that the nuns were much older than any she had seen in the quarters below. Their faces were creased with wrinkles, their eyes were squinted and some noticeably rheumy. Yet their fingers moved with uncanny speed, the gnarled, liver-spotted hands moving with a steady rhythm.

"What are they doing?" asked Maryetta.

"Come and see."

The many pins and bobbins at first seemed in disarray. Then Maryetta could see that there was a pattern to the work—the nuns were making lace.

"Why do they work so hard?" she asked.

"They feel they must earn their keep, I suppose. It is an art, and one I am certain they enjoy. Theirs is a reputation for making the finest ground lace in all of Belgium."

"But they are so old!" protested Maryetta.

"Yes, dear, but wanting to be a part of life even as you and I."

Maryetta loved the way Sister Celeste seemed always to know what was in the hearts of folk.

"I should like to know how to make lace when I am old. It comes out so—elegant!"

"Would you, now?"

"Oh, yes."

Sister Celeste spoke aside to one of the women, who in turn studied the young girl. She arose and indicated that Maryetta should take her place.

Thanking the elderly woman, Maryetta sat down and Sister Celeste placed a board on her lap, instructing as she did so.

"See—wind the thread over the bobbin—and voila! Around the pins on the pattern!"

Maryetta struggled with the multitude of threads, proceeded to stick herself, winced, sucked on her finger, and gamely attacked the project again. She worked in silence for several minutes.

"You do exceedingly well for a beginner," said the patient Celeste.

The old woman nodded her approval, then suddenly turned and walked away, talking to herself. Maryetta wondered silently if she had in some way offended her. In a brief time the nun returned, carrying a well-wrapped package which she held out toward Maryetta.

"Take it," prompted Sister Celeste. "It is a gift!"

Maryetta slowly unwrapped the package and held up a pair of white lace gloves.

"For me?"

"Try them on. She waits to see if they fit."

Maryetta did as she was told, delighted to find that they fit with a possible fraction of an inch for growth. Impulsively she got to her feet and pressed a kiss onto the wrinkled cheek.

"Oh, Sister, I shall cherish them forever! Bless you!"

Sister Celeste added her thanks to Maryetta's and then bowed her way out, taking Maryetta with her. They retraced their steps down the narrow staircase.

At the foot of the stairs, Maryetta saw a very narrow door she had not noticed before. She moved to open it and found herself in bright sunlight and welcome warmth. The portal led to a garden already responding to spring's first enchanting overtures.

"There should be flowers in a few weeks, Maryetta. We shall pick some when they bloom," said Sister Celeste.

"Where does the path go?" asked Maryetta, entranced with the thought of picking flowers. With wistful longing she recalled the times she and her mother had wandered through the yellow star grass, picking blue pasqueflowers, hepatica, wild roses, and violets.

"It winds through the bushes, dear. See? And out the iron gate to the street."

Maryetta had often wondered about the iron gate when she had been out on the street. Now she knew about the garden and more—she knew of a secret way to the outside world. When they turned back she was still pondering the strange fact that over their heads dwelt a colony of elderly nuns.

WHEN SUMMER ARRIVED, MANY of the students whose homes were in Belgium went home for a vacation. As usual, Maryetta remained at the convent. June moved into July and August. Sister Celeste knew that Maryetta leaned on her presence to ease the lonely days.

"Sister, convent life is so cut off from the world. How am I to know what goes on outside?"

"What do you wish to know?"

"America—what goes on there?"

"Well—the War between the States is over."

"Is that all? I mean, what about the rest of the world?"

The sister looked sad.

"There are other wars. It seems to be the way of the world.

Britain and Russia are signing treaties with China. Prussia still quarrels with Austria."

"And my father—" The old hunted animal look crept back into Maryetta's eyes.

"You want to be near him, don't you, child?" The kind sister slipped an arm around the stooping shoulders and continued, "And your mother—you must miss them both."

Maryetta's face clouded, and she spat out her reply.

"Yes, Sister. I do wish to see my father. But my stepmother I wish to see dead!"

Sister Celeste stared at Maryetta. Was this the child she had taken under her wing, favored, dealt kindly with? She had never before seen this expression on her young charge's face.

"Marie! You must not say such things—ever!"

"It is true! If she does not die, I shall never see my father again!"

"But it is a mortal sin to wish anyone dead!"

"I do not care about your mortal sins! I have been treated badly. You cannot know. I have been lied about . . . and abandoned!"

The situation was worse than the good Sister had imagined. Clearly there was a root of bitterness here, and a deformed sapling was about to grow inside this child she loved so dearly. Already poison blossoms were budding.

Sister Celeste could not pursue the situation at the moment, but pursue she must. In silence they walked down the quiet corridor, their pleasant camaraderie destroyed.

Then they turned a corner—and found themselves face to face with Sister Anunciata. Her lips were set harshly, her eyes accusing as she stood studying the two.

"And what is Mademoiselle Marie doing here? She should be in her art class."

Sister Celeste recovered quickly and stood her ground.

"I allow Marie occasional diversion. Summer classes are not that important."

"She will be punished," said the nun in an officious tone.

Maryetta stood unflinching, awaiting her sentence.

Sister Celeste knew instinctively that this was her first test, an opportunity to tear away at the hard shards already sealing Maryetta's heart.

"Some children are very sensitive—" she began, but was cut off.

"Elle est Américaine et protestante. Il n'ya pas de doute, il faut lui enseigner la discipline."

Looking directly at the quarrelsome nun, Sister Celeste spoke quietly but firmly. *"Mais ces enfants ont besoin d'amour."*

Maryetta winced at the harsh judgment, wondering why being an American and a Protestant should merit discipline. She felt a rush of love for her dear champion Sister Celeste for defending her.

Sister Anunciata blanched and then flushed with indignation, then turned and stalked away.

"I am also a stepchild, Sister. Is that as bad as being a Protestant and an American?" she asked Sister Celeste when the two were again alone.

Sister Celeste looked discouraged. She knew that the censuring Sister Anunciata had been at the convent much longer than she and could justifiably say that Celeste had no right to make her own rules.

Maryetta feared she had brought on her dear friend's despondency.

"Why are some folk so mean?" she asked, sighing heavily.

"Keep in mind Marie, that it takes all kinds of people to make a world—even a sisterhood. I fear Sister Anunciata sees herself as God's appointed administrator and judge. She enjoys authority! But I do pray for her."

"You pray for mean people?"

"Always, and you must too."

"You are different, Sister. But then, you are a nun, and God answers the prayers of nuns. He'd never bother with mine."

"Wherever did you get such a notion?"

"Oh, I have prayed—but I wasn't heard. Nuns are different. If their prayers weren't answered, surely they would not keep on as they do."

The sister looked with pity at Maryetta. Indeed, there was work cut out for her here—work that would take time and patience.

"My dear Marie, we mortals cannot presume to know whose prayers our Lord hears. We can only presume that for some reason God desires that we pray. Come to my room and we will pray together."

Maryetta, who would never dream of disobeying her beloved friend, followed and knelt beside her. She watched entranced at the way Sister Celeste seemed to move from the earthly to the heavenlies, wishing desperately that she, too, could change worlds so easily.

TOWARD THE END OF August, Celeste came to Maryetta's room with her hands behind her back and a sparkle in her eyes.

"I have something for you, Marie!"

"A letter? Oh, say it is a letter—please!"

"*Oui, Mademoiselle*—it is a letter!" She held out a small envelope and settled herself beside Maryetta.

Eagerly Maryetta tore at the pink envelope.

"Mercy! Wait! You will tear it to shreds!" exclaimed the Sister, reaching into the pocket of her voluminous skirt and producing a small pen knife. She slit the envelope and handed the letter back to Maryetta.

"It is not from my father," said Maryetta, disappointed and ready to cry.

"But see! You have photographs!"

Indeed, three photographs had spilled out from the envelope and onto the bed. Maryetta at first picked them up with little interest and then suddenly brightened.

"My mother! My real mother! Oh, Sister, these are the pictures my father kept on his desk—until Lydia came."

The nun studied the photograph.

"Yes, Maryetta. On the outside I see some of her beauty in you. But tell me, did she also have the heart of a little tiger on the inside?"

Maryetta looked away from the discerning nun. How was it that the Sister could always strike at the core of things? She watched as Sister Celeste picked up the second photograph.

"Who is this, Marie?"

"It is also my mother. She was more grown up in this one."

"And this one—what a darling little girl. My! Someone liked photographs!"

"My father believed one should always take advantage of new inventions. I guess you could say he appreciated anything to do with pioneering. I remember when that one was taken of me. The dress was old-rose, the lace black. Wasn't that dreadful for one so young?"

The sister studied Maryetta.

"I think you have your father's eyes. But come—read your letter."

"It seems to be from my Ellen. I do not read English very fast. Would you read it for me, please?"

Obligingly Celeste began.

My dear little Maryetta,

I am sorry I have not written more, but circumstances have changed for me, and I have almost nothing that resembles money. When your new mama came back from Europe it was in a good frame of mind, but after a few weeks she found so much fault with me that I up and left. It was no use trying to please her. When I left, I helped myself to the photographs so you could have them. Your mother's was in the old trunk and I did not trust Mrs. Lydia to keep them, nor would she ever send them to you.

I found a good family to work for, though they don't have much of this world's goods. Still, they offered me a room of my own and food, which is a good deal to one of my station and age. I am appreciated—which is all a body could ask.

Your papa survived the terrible war, but I feel sorry for him. He made a dreadful mistake marrying Mrs. Lydia and he is trying to make the best of it. He keeps very busy with his patients. When I left, he promised to come see me and he does occasionally. The last time I saw him, he expressed his shame at neglecting you. He did this very contritely, so try not to bear him ill will. Pray for him as I do.

He speaks of going to California, opening sanitariums for the poor folk with tuberculosis. You will be glad to know I took Tishme with me. She grows old for a cat, but she knows I will always care for her. Now please write to me so I'll know you are alive. I miss you more than words can tell.

Affectionately,
Your Ellen MacDougal

Sister Celeste put the letter down, pleased with its contents. She was unprepared for the burst of tears that followed. Gently she cradled the weeping girl, forgoing any words until the outburst subsided.

"Tell me more about Tishme," she asked, hoping to turn Maryetta's thoughts to better things.

Between sobs, Maryetta managed to speak.

"She was my beautiful cat. Father brought her to me when we lived in Iowa." And she told her friend how the kitten got her name, laughing chokingly through her tears. "I wish I could see her."

"You must be grateful that your Ellen has her, Marie. God does have concern even for little animals."

"Yes, Sister. I am grateful, but being grateful doesn't help the awful feelings I have down deep inside. Do you think I shall ever feel right—have some of my questions answered?"

"Yes, Marie, I am sure the day will come when you will see that our God does care—and how very much."

6

By the time another summer came around, Maryetta had learned not only to appreciate the fellowship of the other nuns at the convent, but the camaraderie of her young school friends. Since she could know nothing of the pleasures of a visit home, she devoured the tales of family life that Antoinette brought back with her. The girls would sit for hours with Maryetta drinking in recitations of picnics, parties, and outings. Janine, too, always returned at summer's end with a collection of humorous stories.

At times during the long summer, Sister Celeste would come to Maryetta's room and read to her in the evenings, the sound of her beautiful French blessing Maryetta's ears.

Sometimes Sister Josephine took her to the market near the Grand Place, and with Sister Agnes she could go to the market of St. Catherine to purchase the newly arrived vegetables and fruit.

They left always with the admonition from Sister Anunciata that they patronize only shops that displayed the sign of the Chanticleer, avoiding all commerce with Les Flamands.

It had often puzzled Maryetta that such commerce was forbidden. The obvious antagonism was reflected in the separate communities as well as in separate newspapers. She could not know that the history of the little country had spawned inner rivalries, that William of Orange had made so many anti-Catholic laws that the Walloons had revolted. Later industrial advantages in Walloon country had brought the French language into dominance as well as into the school system, which of course was savagely rejected by the Flemish population.

"Why do we avoid Les Flamands?" she asked Sister Agnes as they walked along.

"Because—" Sister Agnes hesitated, looking perplexed. "Well, because—they are not Walloons!" Her tone indicated that anyone with an ounce of sense should know that.

Chestnut trees were in full bloom, and the city's parks were setting forth their exquisite beauty. Maryetta ran from one blooming *parterre* to another. The bright colors were like the flagrantly colored fabrics the vendors displayed at the little shops—all so enchanting and so different from the drab walls of the convent. Tantalizing aromas drifted from the bakery, provocative in the morning air and making Maryetta wonder what special treat the jolly proprietor would place on the high counter for her this day.

She appreciated most the days of summer, the release from strict schedules and the opportunity to be in the out-of-doors. Once she asked Sister Agnes if they might someday visit the bird market of which she had heard so many glowing tales. She was indignantly reproved. The bird market was open only on weekends. Saturdays were for cleaning rooms and Sundays were to be kept holy. The denial only piqued Maryetta's curiosity more, and secretly she vowed that she most certainly would see the bird market some day!

The denial, however, was somewhat assuaged, for the good prioress was more than anxious to educate her small charges, particularly in the arts. She herself took the children to view the great masterpieces of which her city could boast, including Rubens's "Adoration of the Magi" and Jordaens's "Allegory of Fecundity."

They visited the grand cathedrals, standing entranced before the stained-glass windows, awed at the high-groined arches, the statuary, the magnificent choir lofts. Maryetta felt the antiquity and sacrosanctity of the place. Here, it seemed, were enshrined the vestiges of the little country's illustrious past—the grandeur of Gothic architecture and the remnant evidences of dukes and

Spanish Hapsburgs. The excursions did much to help Maryetta appreciate and understand the diversities of the country's people.

Their days were not restricted to learning. The children who had to remain at the convent through the summer months because of their distance from home were often treated to a day of travel, a picnic, or the rare privilege of watching schools of summer artists, each with his musette bag and well-chosen paints, as they tried to capture on canvas some of the quaint scenes of the city.

By September, the visionary Sister Celeste had arranged for Maryetta to study piano. Strangely, the money was always there when there was an opportunity to increase her abilities. Maryetta wondered if it were evidence of her father's salving his conscience or a means of inflating Lydia's pride, allowing her to boast of their daughter's advantages in the social world. In either case, she would not be employed to use her talents to please her parents. It was the beloved Sister she sought to please.

CHRISTMAS WAS AT HAND once again, and by now the little tryst that had been inaugurated five years ago had become an annual celebration. This year the affair was a little more festive than usual, for Celeste had decorated her room and, in place of the Greek bread, had purchased little cream cakes—*creme de beurre,* she called them. But more significant than the rare delicacies was the knowledge to Maryetta that she had a special place in the heart of another.

The elderly nuns had taught her how to edge handkerchiefs and make doilies, so she was able to present her dear benefactress with a small token of her deep affection. Sister Celeste gushed over the belabored gifts as only she could, making Maryetta beam with pride.

The evening ended with the Sister singing a little French song, a song she said she had learned in her childhood. It was a composition that had sprung from the agile mind of an eighteenth-century artist, and she sang it with surprising gusto, tapping her toes to its martial tempo.

The Sister's eyes sparkled as she sang, and Maryetta wondered if she, too, had memories of loved ones from whom she had been separated by strange circumstances.

BY AGE FIFTEEN, MARYETTA had been appointed companion to Sister Celeste when she was sent on errands. She was taken on excursions with the beloved sister to many little sidewalk restaurants, often to secluded spots for a picnic by small streams where they might toss crumbs to hungry ducks. But best of all were the shared secrets of the heart, the getting to know one another.

Once again Maryetta asked if she might visit the bird market.

"But it is open only on Saturday and Sunday, child. You know we aren't allowed such privileges on the Holy Sabbath, and on Saturday we must clean!"

Maryetta's disappointment showed on her face, and the gentle sister reached a comforting hand toward her.

"Cheer up, little one. I will try to think of a way."

A month passed, and one bright sunny Sunday, the sister approached her.

"Today I have arranged that we visit the church of St. Gudule."

Something in the nun's expression told Maryetta she was holding back something of extreme importance.

"Just you and I?" she asked.

"Yes, dear. You have not seen the glasswork of Van Orley. The Mother thinks it time to show you some of the chapel's treasures."

Maryetta dressed quickly and joined her friend. Through a little park and down a slope they walked together until they came to the church, where they sat through a lengthy mass. When they emerged into the bright sunlight of the day, they crossed several streets. Maryetta could see the tall Guild Houses and knew they were close to the Grand Place—and the bird market!

"We shall stop at the bird market—but not for long," said the sister, stealing a glance at her charge.

Maryetta smiled slowly, beginning to see through her friend's subtlety.

They entered the little avenues made by the stacked cages. Maryetta walked up and down the colorful array of strange birds, enthralled with their squawking and scolding. The white canaries delighted her most and surprised her that they could sing so boisterously in their cramped cages.

She was unaware that she was being observed by the owner and his wife until they approached her. He spoke in Dutch-Flemish, a language she had heard only occasionally. She turned a bewildered glance in the Sister's direction.

"What does he say, Sister?"

"He asks if you like his birds."

Looking the man over, Maryetta decided he was quite harmless. He was short and fair, with a pleasant face. A shock of straw-colored hair poked from beneath his round, black cap. His eyes were small triangles and had a trace of humor in them, his nose was pudgy, and something about him indicated a hidden intelligence.

"Answer him, Maryetta!" prodded the Sister, standing politely aside.

Maryetta's expression showed her confusion. How could she answer him if she could not speak his language?

"I will interpret," offered Celeste.

"Oui, Monsieur—" said Maryetta, then turned helplessly back to Sister Celeste. "Ask him his name. I do not know how to address him!"

The nun spoke to the man in the same strange tongue, and Maryetta marveled at her versatility. Did she know every language of the continent?

"He says you are not to call him monsieur. His name is Emile Goette."

"But how do I preface his name?"

"You might try Mijnheer Goette."

That settled, Maryetta spoke directly to the merchant. *"Oui,* Mijnheer Goette," she said with a winning smile.

He looked unhappy with her mixed response.

"Why does he insist that I speak in another language? Does he not understand French?"

"He is Fleming. Can you not tell by his appearance?"

"He seems angry. Doesn't he like Les Walloons?"

"No more than the Walloons like Les Flamands!"

"How ridiculous—and all Belgians! Isn't it dreadful, Sister, that there must be divisions in God's world?"

The man spoke again.

"What does he say now?"

"He invites you to visit in his home sometime and to view his young canaries. He says some are still eggs."

"May I go?"

"Not today, but perhaps sometime."

The man's wife spoke up. "I spik some *Anglais*—you are Catholic student?" she asked in broken English.

"I am a student, yes," answered Maryetta, "but I am not Catholic. I am Presbyterian."

They talked briefly, and then the little woman wrote out directions to her home, which Maryetta tucked in her pocket with a polite thank-you.

THE SUMMER PASSED SWIFTLY, and with autumn just around the corner Maryetta wondered if she would ever see the Goettes' young canaries. When it grew cold, the birds would be taken away, and she feared she would not see them or their owners again. She lay awake many a night wishing she might accept the Goettes' invitation and wondering how she could possibly leave the convent alone to satisfy her curiosity.

Then she remembered the narrow door at the foot of the garret stairs. Sister Celeste had said that the garden path led to the street. If that were so, why could she not make an attempt to visit the Goettes by herself? She could slip out at night. If she planned it well, her absence would never be discovered. The scrap of paper with the directions to the Goettes was hidden away in a winter coat pocket. Whenever Maryetta had a few free moments, she studied the simple map and in no time committed it to memory.

For a number of days the rains of autumn had soaked the earth, announcing that the onslaught of winter was close at hand. Maryetta could wait no longer. Carefully she laid her plans.

The front doors were locked, the washing, the brushing, and the prayers had brought the day to an end. With most of the wall candles extinguished, the girls had settled down for a night's sleep. But not Maryetta! Anticipating the adventure that lay ahead, and with her senses galvanized, she could not possibly sleep.

She lay silently listening until she was certain her peers were asleep. She had no idea of the time when she decided to make her move. Noiselessly she arose, dressed quickly, and moved out into the silent corridor. Regularly she hid in the *intrados,* standing in the recessed alcoves and listening for possible hindrances. Reaching the narrow door at the foot of the garret steps, she slipped outside and into the dark garden. Raindrops dampened her clothing as she brushed past the garden shrubbery, but she was soon on the street with quickened step and heartbeat.

She followed the memorized directions and soon found herself knocking on the door of the Goettes.

Mevrouw Goette opened the door and stood looking in surprise at the wide-eyed girl facing her. Recovering, she invited Maryetta inside.

"You, Maryetta!" she exclaimed.

"Yes."

"You com at nacht?" she asked. "Vy not daytime?"

"I have come the only time I could—to see the baby canaries."

Maryetta could see Mijnheer Goette seated at a roughly carved dining table. He arose quickly when he recognized Maryetta, looked her over with curiosity and spoke to his wife. Whatever she said in response seemed to please him.

"Com," said Mevrouw Goette, "My husbint invite you to dine."

"Dank u zeer," said Maryetta politely, grateful that Sister Celeste

had taught her a few polite expressions in Flemish.

Mijnheer Goette was already ladling green soup into a beautiful blue bowl for her, while his wife vigorously cut thick slices of bread from what appeared to be a hard crusted loaf. She placed a piece of apple and cheese on the same blue-patterned dish. Passing her the plate, the man waited to see if Maryetta would bow her head. He seemed gratified and pleased when she did.

"They let you go out at nacht—alone?" asked the woman.

Maryetta thought it best just to nod, and they went on eating.

Mijnheer Goette finished first, waited until the others were done, and then arose. He walked to a long wall table where he picked up a very large Bible from its favored place among the couple's earthly treasures. The man's absorbed interest in the pages he turned gave Maryetta an opportunity to look around the room.

The cleanliness of the place was impressive. There were waxed wooden bowls on a chiffonier, and on a polished wooden hutch sat an entire set of lovely Delftware. Surely it must have been an heirloom treasure! Fresh white curtains hung at casement windows, and Maryetta could imagine the sunlight of day striking the homey kitchen scene—a scene not unlike the paintings of Pieter De Hooch.

She had not felt so much at home since leaving the old Iowa cabin, and the memory of her tired mother lifting kettles too heavy for her strength swept in upon Maryetta.

The observant Mijnheer noticed Maryetta struggling to hold back her tears, and he spoke sharply to his wife. She, in turn, moved toward Maryetta.

"You are troubled?" asked the little woman.

Maryetta dabbed at her eyes with a handkerchief and pretended not to hear. Perhaps her weakness would go unnoticed if she could control her ridiculous thoughts and unwelcome tears.

"Speak up, child," said her hostess.

Glancing swiftly in the direction of the little Flem, Maryetta saw only her beloved Ellen, and the tears she had meant to control suddenly spilled over.

Instantly the good woman was beside her and her arms were around her.

"You are not happy at the convent?" she asked.

"I am not unhappy there. It is just that—my father—"

"Does he not visit you?"

"He has forgotten me," answered Maryetta.

"That could not be," soothed the woman.

"It is true—but forgive me. I had no intention of speaking about it. I really came to see your canaries."

Mevrouw Goette filled her husband in on the conversation. He looked kindly at Maryetta and spoke again in Flemish.

"My husbint says you shall see his birts—but first—we are to encourage you."

The man was turning the pages of his big Bible and talking away as though Maryetta understood his every word. His wife smiled at Maryetta, sharing her amusement at his naiveté.

"What does he say?" asked Maryetta, now put at ease in the company of the kind couple.

"He says—'Wort of Gott'—his best food."

Maryetta made a wry face. "What a funny thing to say."

He went on speaking and his wife interpreted.

"He say, we should everyone know the Wort of Gott—someday we be judged by it."

"Gracious! And I have never read it!" exclaimed Maryetta.

For some reason, Mijnheer Goette understood that! He looked sadly at Maryetta and then at his wife, instructing her to interpret what he read aloud.

"The answers are here—the answers to problems—now—Joseph!"

Mevrouw Goette interpreted as her husband read.

"You should know of Joseph. He be treated bad by his jealous brudders. Sold to slave traders—taken off to a foreign land—like you—forgotten—but not by his fadder—and not by his Gott. After long time his fadder come to Egypt with the brudders—and

Joseph—he forgiff. He say, 'You mean it for eefil—but Gott mean it for goot.' "

"I shall never forgive!" declared Maryetta.

"Then you grow bitter," said the woman.

The man was still turning the pages.

"He now read about Ruth," said the wife.

This Maryetta listened to with interest. "Call me Mara, for the Lord has dealt bitterly with me." Ah, she could relate to that woman. She savored the name—Mara—not too different from her own Maryetta . . . Marie!

Mijnheer Goette closed the Bible and arose.

"We go see canaries now," said his wife. She smiled and placed her arm around Maryetta.

The back room seemed to be his place of operation, for cages were all around the room. He whistled and talked, awakening them from their early roosting. He muttered something about *eieren*, and his wife explained that he was counting eggs.

"Ve haf much eggs a'ready," she said.

The man was already lifting his treasured eggs with a teaspoon, which he repeatedly heated over a candle flame. Then he was on to the task of mashing the yolk of hard-boiled eggs and stuffing tiny mouths.

Maryetta glanced at a wall clock and gasped.

"I must go!" She turned back to the front room and headed for the door.

Mevrouw Goette hurried after her, and Mijnheer followed.

"You com back?" asked the woman, worry pinching her brow.

"I do not know," answered Maryetta, marveling that she had even managed to visit the good people in the first place. "It is not easy."

"Ve pray for you," assured the woman, squeezing Maryetta's hand affectionately.

"Thank you—and *tot ziens*."

With no more ado, Maryetta stepped out into the late night and hurried along the dark street toward the convent. When she reached the garden, she breathed a sigh of relief. The gate and the little narrow door were still open, the corridors as silent and as absent of life as when she had left them. She had no problem returning to her room and to her bed.

She did not sleep, however, but lay awake thinking of the things she had heard and seen. Close to dawn she fell asleep and dreamed of yellow and white canaries and blue Delftware. But most of all, she saw the face of a young Jewish lad who had been rudely taken from his family to a strange country.

She awoke still hugging to her breast the sorrow Joseph must have felt . . . and still remembering a name she could easily adopt. Mara . . . Mara. . . . How well it suited her!

7

THE YEARS MOVED ON. IN SPITE OF SISTER CELESTE'S LABORS OF kindness, the deep-seated wound of her father's broken promise still festered in Maryetta's heart. With each new return of spring, hope stirred that this might be her last year of exile, that on one fine morning a call would come for her to go to the office of the prioress and her very own Papa would be standing there with his arms outstretched. She would run into them and he would plant a bewhiskered kiss on her cheek and the loneliness would be forever gone.

But with the leaves of October her hopes would come falling down, and with the winter snows they were buried. Cold chilled the land and the heart.

Prussia's Iron Chancellor Otto von Bismarck was pursuing his dictatorial conviction that "Blood and Iron" alone could solve the problems of his Emperor. Belgium's Leopold II was at the same time casting covetous eyes upon the wealth of the African continent.

European financiers were also awakening to the assiduous inventive prowess of young Americans. They could see opportunities for gain and good fortune by promoting the young nation's industries. The phenomenal upsurge of emigration, too, with the promise of cheap labor was beginning to send European dollars to the new country. Partnerships were evolving into corporations, poolings, trusts, mergers, and amalgamations.

Letters came from Ellen and Aunt Miriam, telling Maryetta of her father's travels and frequent separations from the scheming Lydia. He was now considered a real pioneer in recuperative medicine. The news at first gave Maryetta some pleasure, but that soon dissipated. The wife's loss was no gain for the daughter! She was glad he had survived the terrible war, but what about his promise to come for her? Had he forgotten? Had he really stopped caring?

By 1867 Maryetta at age fifteen had changed outwardly. Gone now were the angular features, the gangling arms and legs of the adolescent, and in their place were the soft, curving contours of the full-grown woman.

Under the nurturing care of Sister Celeste a flicker of confidence was emerging. Maryetta had been given responsibilities that were beginning to establish some worth both within herself and to those around her. She was now given the duty of welcoming the young children sent from America. It was a position of trust and respect, but more than that a blessing, for Maryetta of all people could relate to the fears and the loneliness of these little ones.

For those so fortunate to have homes in or near Belgium, vacation time was once again on the horizon. Stoically, as was Maryetta's mindset by now, she had accepted the fact that for her there would be no returning home. Instead she made herself available to her peers, helping them pack for the coveted event.

When their time of departure drew near, their jubilance developed into hysteria. Names such as Bruges, Ghent, Oostende, and Charleroi could be heard as they packed and chattered.

It was in the midst of such preparation that the sandy-haired Antoinette approached the solemn-faced American girl.

"Marie, may I ask a special favor—and please do not say no until you have thought about it."

Maryetta was sure she was being asked to help with Antoinette's packing and smiled reassuringly, giving her classmate the encouragement to continue.

"If I were to invite you to my home, would you come? We both know you have never had a vacation. It would do you good. And it would be good for me, too."

Maryetta flushed and struggled to hide her surprise. To be included, wanted, seemed too good to be true. But she must not be too obvious—to show her feelings was unthinkable. She must demur, pretend she needed time to consider the invitation.

"That would be very nice, Antoinette. I will ask if the Mother can spare me."

The prioress could indeed spare Maryetta, agreeing with Antoinette that a vacation would do the young American a great deal of good.

"You have excelled in your school work, Maryetta, and you should be rewarded." She smiled at the girl. "I think I can manage your duties for a brief time."

Maryetta hastened to Antoinette with the news, and the packing took on a vibrant gaiety.

THE JOSEPH DE LA MARQUES LIVED near the seaport of Oostende where Antoinette's father owned a lively shipping business. He had promised to send the family carriage to fetch the girls, and its arrival early one morning caused quite a stir among the remaining students.

A portly coachman sat erect in his crimson uniform, reins in one hand and a whip in the other. Beside him sat a footman, stiff and proper.

Sister Celeste saw the girls to the carriage in an ebullient state, sending them off with a kiss and her blessing. They traveled along the road, rolling and pitching, feeling like the royal family themselves. They viewed the changing scenery and stopped at major cities, enjoying the hubbub of European cosmopolitanism and stopping to eat *gaufres* and change horses at small inns. It was not long before the excitement and the weight of traveling hours began to be felt. Nodding from the constant rocking of the carriage, the two fell easily into a deep sleep.

A sudden change in the horses' gait awoke them, and they could see in the twilighted distance the twin spires of Saints Peter and Paul. The air, too, had changed, flooding the carriage with a sweet sea-blown freshness. They traveled awhile through the streets of Oostende, and then the coachman turned the horses' heads in a southwesterly direction. Then turning sharply at a wide, pillared entrance, they came to an abrupt stop before a palatial dwelling.

Antoinette's parents came down the steps and greeted them warmly. Maryetta was led into the lavish interior where statuette and Louis XIV furniture abounded. Staring awestruck at the luxury of the rich surroundings, she suddenly recalled Tishme stepping off the heavy carpeting of their New York home.

Both girls went directly to their separate rooms, where servants were quick to bring them warm water and clean towels before a late supper.

At the table, Antoinette talked animatedly with her parents, describing her life at the convent school. Maryetta sat apart from the laughter and the storytelling, wondering at the sweet camaraderie of the family and silencing as best she could the inner voice of covetousness. She busied herself with the gourmet courses so artistically served by uniformed servants; *Bisque de Homard, croquette aux crevettes*, and fruit from Dinant.

Taking note of the weariness on the girls' faces, Antoinette's parents excused them promptly with a promise of pleasant days to come.

The habit of early rising, the sun at the windows, and Antoinette at the foot of her bed brought Maryetta from a deep sleep.

"Come! We go horseback riding!"

Maryetta sleepily pushed the invitation aside. "I am not certain I remember how to ride," she protested.

"But you must! It is like swimming, Marie. You do not forget."

Doubtfully, but not wishing to offend her young hostess, Maryetta arose.

"Here—I have brought you my brother's clothes. We will be at the shore and could get wet. See! I dress casually, too!" And the enthusiastic Antoinette spun around to display her male attire.

They joined the livery attendants and were soon up on their steeds and heading toward the ocean. The beach stretched as far as Maryetta could see, and there were other early riders scattered along the sandy strand. Fishermen, too, were astride heavy horses, snaring the *crevettes* for the seaside vendors.

Breathing deeply of the fresh salt air, Maryetta began to relax and even be glad she had come.

Having gained her objective, Antoinette now sought her own pleasure. Spurring her mount, she took off at a healthy gallop, the patronizing attendant in hot pursuit. If it had been meant as a challenge to her schoolmate, it had gone for naught. For Maryetta, just to be riding beside the sea on a beautiful summer morning was enough.

She rode for awhile, then reined in her horse, gently released the horse weight, and dropped down upon the sand. Walking toward the lapping waves, she looked into the heavens. Something in the cry of the gulls stirred memories, brought into dull focus a time when her father had introduced her to Maine's seacoast, so long ago that she could scarcely remember. But she could hear the dashing waves and feel again the rough wool of her father's shirt as she leaned against him—feel the protective arms, see the ears of a gray horse bobbing in front of them and the pleasant rocking in the saddle. Yes, she could remember that—and want it.

Overcome with the flash of memory, she walked into the water without thinking.

"Somewhere out there—across this very sea—is my home—my own country—my own father! Oh, Lord, if you see me at all, please give me an answer. Tell me, how long will You keep me here?"

Trembling, she fell to her knees, not even feeling the water, and sobbing as she spoke aloud.

"Father—Father. Oh, why have you forsaken me?"

"Pardon me, young miss. Are you all right?"

The voice was a man's, the accent distinctly British.

Maryetta turned, straining through her tears to see who had spoken. Hastily she got to her feet, crimson with embarrassment at having been overheard.

Who was this stranger? As her eyes cleared she could see that his gray hair had once been a pale sorrel. His well-tanned face bespoke many years of living close to the shore. His eyes were a pale blue, wide set and gentle . . . as a father's should be.

She stammered out an apology for her outburst and headed for her mount.

Ignoring her attempt to flee, the stranger quickly followed.

"I could not help overhearing. Has your father left you?"

How could she possibly explain—and why should she? She had been taught that young ladies did not speak to strangers.

He, on the other hand, seemed to know nothing of such gentility and went on speaking.

"It is so strange!"

"Sir?"

"Just this morning I preached a sermon on those very words!"

"What words, sir?"

"Jesus' words—asking His father why He had forsaken Him."

"Jesus asked that?"

"Surely you know."

"No, sir, I do not know. Tell me."

"When He was dying in our place—you have heard that—and felt forsaken. It is often that way, the darkest before the dawn. His dawn came three days later, when no one dreamed it could. Whatever the problem, one must hope, for there is always an Easter for the faithful."

"You are a Protestant clergyman?"

"Nigel Edmunds is my name. And yours?"

"I am Maryetta Cobbet. I live at a convent in Brussels."

"You are Catholic?"

"No, sir, I am Presbyterian. My mother and father were both Presbyterian."

"Then what are you doing in a Catholic convent?"

Maryetta sighed. "It is a long story."

"But you feel forsaken."

"I am forsaken!"

"Then you must pray."

"I did at first, but God hears only the prayers of nuns . . . and maybe men like you. He doesn't even know me."

"Oh, but He does, I assure you. He knows all about you. Have you never heard of His omniscience?"

"Sister Celeste said something about that."

"And who is Sister Celeste?"

"She is the dearest person on earth. I could not live without Sister Celeste!"

"I see. God must have sent her to you."

The thought was comforting, and Maryetta studied the man again.

"Where is your parish, Mr.—?"

"Edmunds," he supplied. He smiled affably. "My parish—now don't laugh, and don't judge me a thief, for I steal the phrase from a great preacher of the past—the world is my parish."

Maryetta did not understand. "What do you do in Oostende?" she asked.

"I have a ministry with seamen. Sometimes here, sometimes over the channel."

"Have you not the education to pastor a real parish?"

"I told you. I have a real parish."

Maryetta shook her head. The man made little sense. And here were Antoinette and her attendant heading back, their horses now walking at a relaxed gait.

The stranger's words about Easter made Maryetta want to talk longer, but she could see little opportunity.

"I should like to talk longer, but my hostess is coming back. I am a guest at the Joseph de la Marque villa."

"Will you be riding tomorrow?"

"Possibly."

"Then I shall meet you."

Riding back to the villa, Maryetta cast about in her mind the strange meeting and the man's words. Where had she seen him before—or had she? He reminded her of something she had seen in the face of Sister Celeste. She must speak to the sister about that, when she returned to the convent.

THE DAYS THAT FOLLOWED at the big house were memorable indeed. Truly, the outside world had its fun and its attraction, but it did not offer the peace her heart craved.

She became increasingly curious about Mr. Edmunds's ministry and made a decided effort to see him again, being careful to excuse herself from Antoinette's company.

She found the clergyman true to his word, waiting each morning to meet her. As the sun dispels the darkness of night, so with his words there returned a glimmer of hope that there could be better days ahead for her. He continued to say with such certainty that God knew about her predicament that Maryetta could not ignore him.

Each morning he opened his Bible and taught her. First it was the genealogy of Jesus' mother, for he saw that his young friend needed to realize the humanity of Jesus as well as His divinity.

"I like to read the Gospel of Luke. So plainly written. Have you ever read the doctor's gospel? I am sure he must have spent a lot of time like a newspaper reporter, getting all of his facts—visiting and interviewing Mary and the others. He must have heard the Magnificat right from her own lips."

Maryetta enjoyed the way this man seemed on such intimate terms with the Holy Scriptures. He took her as a visitor back to the little towns of the Bible—to the desert places—to the synagogue—to the temple.

"Maryetta, this Jesus was sent especially to you. Listen to this!" And he read, "The Spirit of the Lord is upon me, because he hath appointed me to preach the gospel to the poor; he hath sent me to heal the brokenhearted, to preach deliverance to the captives, and recovering of sight to the blind, to set at liberty them that are bruised."

How was it that words spoken so long ago could have healing for the bruised of her day? Could the great and holy God really set her at liberty? Truly, there was something to that, for as Nigel Edmunds spoke she felt a loosening of the grasp someone or something had on her. Could she dare to believe that God had kept His word for people as in need as she was herself?

Mr. Edmunds read the questions in her eyes.

"Take it to yourself, Maryetta. Believe in this Jesus. Believe in His death for you, in His everlasting love and concern for you—His Easter, His overcoming, and His words. Reach out for His promises. Reach out, Maryetta, and find Him to be everything you need."

Maryetta hesitated, an inborn honesty holding her back. Knowing that believing would also carry responsibilities, knowing her heart should be pure. . . .

She was convinced that never, never would she be rid of her dark and murderous hatred for Lydia. It would always be with her. She even took pleasure in her plans to return someday and make her stepmother suffer as much as the woman had made her suffer. She would repay this person who had lied about her, brought about the estrangement from her father, banished her to a foreign country.

Maryetta pulled back.

"I do not believe I can do that, sir. Perhaps another time, but not now."

She had expected the minister to press, but he did not. Instead, he said good-bye.

She watched soberly as he walked away. Up over a slight rise and into a brilliant morning sun he walked until all she could see was his silhouette.

When she returned to the beach the next day she did not find him, and she felt alone and dispirited. Yet his words remained. He had promised her an Easter—and she wanted that more than anything in life.

Back at the convent, kneeling at the prayer bench with her peers, Maryetta could look upon the crucified Christ with the knowledge that He had had an Easter . . . and she might too.

8

THE CONVENT WITH ALL OF ITS AUSTERITY, ITS UNCOMPROMISING rules, and its regimented life-style, was proving a bulwark against the idiosyncrasies of a constantly changing world. Maryetta more and more appreciated the protection it afforded her. Too, it was giving her an advantage in education, and she was wise enough to apply herself and give her studies first priority.

Carefully she had locked away the anger and bitterness spawned by her stepmother. Yes, it was still there—but well hidden. She was determined to prove to herself, more than to others, that she would not be a victim of circumstances all of her life!

Nigel Edmunds had assured her that she was definitely considered by the living God. The clergyman had planted a seedling of hope, and now Maryetta could experience her own colloquies with the unseen God—ask Him questions and expect answers—approach Him the way she had always wanted to.

"I do believe you are learning to pray, Marie," commented Sister Celeste after observing Maryetta at chapel prayers.

"I talk to God," answered Maryetta tacitly.

"What prayers do you use?"

"I am sorry, Sister. I do not use Catholic prayers. Somehow I think if I were God, I would not care to hear what belonged to another. It is too much like offering Him leftovers or hand-me-downs."

"Marie!"

"Well . . . that is how I feel. Is that wrong?"

Sister Celeste sighed heavily. "Child, you mystify me! Are you an angel or a renegade?"

Maryetta faced her mentor.

"Well, you tell me. What am I? Who am I? Am I really Maryetta, or am I Marie Corbay? Sometimes I think I am both. I really never wanted to be more than Maryetta. I would have liked to remain Maryetta. But perhaps—"Maryetta looked wistfully beyond her friend "—perhaps it is best to settle for Mara. More fitting than either, don't you agree?"

The nun studied Maryetta, wondering where she had learned of the scriptural Mara. Crossing to where the girl stood and taking her firmly by the shoulders, Sister Celeste spoke solemnly.

"Do you not know, my dear one, that Mara must die before Maryetta can live?"

Maryetta turned away from the searching eyes, and Sister Celeste went on.

"I hope you have forgiven your stepmother, because if you have not, it is you who will suffer and not she. Remember, she feels nothing. It is you who carry the thorn in your heart."

Maryetta frowned, not at what the dear Sister had said, but at the dreadful possibility that she had in some way disappointed Sister Celeste.

"Oh, Sister," she cried, "how can you possibly know the rage that goes on inside of me? You have nothing of evil in you!"

Sister Celeste hesitated. The young girl's need was so apparent, but dare she bare her own heart?

"Perhaps . . . just perhaps . . . I do know. Perhaps I have not always been as you know me now."

Maryetta's interest was stirred. This lovely person could never have been anything but perfect.

"Perhaps I was as errant as any other until, like Magdalene of old, I stopped long enough to look into the face of Jesus Christ and see myself as He saw me."

Maryetta was abashed. "You did that?"

"Perhaps . . . I did . . . perhaps I went straight to the truth and threw myself on His mercy. I did not know it at the time, but that was all He required. As time passed, I felt myself changing. There is healing in a broken and a contrite spirit. I recommend it to every troubled soul. There is forgiveness and there is healing . . . and God bestows power to change and to enter into new life."

Maryetta pondered this strange conversation for days.

THE YOUNG STUDENTS BEGAN arriving, and the autumn days of 1867 moved ahead with an air of expectancy. There were new teachers and new classes.

Already the festivals were under way. The Belgians with their love for pageantry and processions cherished as much great musical events. Though they had not given to the world many great composers, they nevertheless opened their doors and hearts to the continent's most gifted artists, flocking to the music halls and conservatories and generously applauding the "foreigners."

From the time of Gregory, music had been a part of the church. Several sisters had attended special concerts and returned to the convent exclaiming over a certain French-born concert pianist from America.

Sister Celeste made plans with Sister Josephine to go and hear him. Several days before they were to go, Sister Celeste complained of a severe headache. When Maryetta expressed concern, her friend made light of it.

"I shall be fine in a few days," she said cheerfully.

But she was not. The headaches persisted.

One afternoon Maryetta received a summons to go to Sister Celeste's room.

"I have requested, Marie, that you go with Sister Josephine to the concert in my place. You are doing well with your music, and you would appreciate hearing such a gifted pianist."

Sister Celeste spoke with difficulty, mentioning that her back ached and that she was suffering from frequent nosebleeds. She said also that she was canceling her classes until she felt better.

"I would much prefer to stay and help you, Sister, if you don't mind. Though I do thank you."

"No, Marie. It is already settled."

"But—"

"Hush! You will disappoint me if you refuse."

"Oh, Sister. You know I could never do that. It's only that I wish you were able to go."

The evening arrived and Maryetta appeared at the sister's door.

"How do I look?" she asked, spinning around to show off a pale-blue dress trimmed with a dark-blue sash and ornamented with narrow blue velvet ribbons. "Antoinette has insisted I borrow her dress—and I shall wear my lace gloves!"

The nun slowly arose from her narrow bed and reached for a rose. Lifting it from its vase, she pinned it to Marie's dress.

"I found a late bloom in the garden. God must have stirred it to grow just for this occasion."

Pressing her nose into the tight blossom, Maryetta drank deeply of its fragrance and planted a kiss on Celeste's cheek.

IT WAS THE SEASON of the *Braderie Bruegel* and music could be heard on every street corner. Maryetta realized she had not been out at night on the streets of Brussels since her secret visit to the Goettes. Suddenly there was magic in the air.

When they arrived at the Conservatoire, folk were already taking their seats and the orchestra was tuning. Maryetta and Sister Josephine found their places just as the lights dimmed.

The conductor came on stage and stood for an enchanted moment with his baton held high. With invigorated bravura he swept it downward. Music such as Maryetta had never heard filled the room, leaving her open-mouthed and staring.

The overture came to an end, and the audience was introduced to the evening's special guest. Maryetta watched spellbound as the celebrated pianist bowed and took his seat. His was a handsome face, and his entire mien charismatic. He was dressed impeccably.

Then his hands were on the keyboard, and she ceased to notice his appearance. The first notes were sharp, startling—seeming to answer to something angry inside of him. He moved with a vitality overwhelming to the young girl's mind, first playing Beethoven's "Adagio Sostemento," then on to Chopin's "Military Polonaise."

On and on the music went, with its own language speaking to the inner soul and sending rapturous tears down Maryetta's face. With a gay glibness, the pianist played the "Emperor's Waltz." When he stopped there was silence, a spellbound moment before the audience could tear itself from the sublime back to the ordinary and mundane.

There was a brief intermission, then the performer returned to play more rousing music. When he stopped, the audience was on its feet. It seemed they could not let him go, so obligingly he sat down and began to play the winsome notes of Beethoven's "Für Elise." Somehow he seemed detached from his audience, playing for himself, moving from performance to a rare intimacy with the music.

The last notes faded away, and he arose and walked to center stage, where he bowed several times. Then the young pianist did something unusual—how like an American!—and the Belgians received it enthusiastically. He asked for a show of hands of the young people present who were in their first two years of piano study. Close to thirty hands shot up. He then invited the novices onstage so he might meet them.

"You must go, Maryetta," encouraged Sister Josephine.

"Oh, no, Sister! He could not possibly care to meet me!"

"He might be pleased to hear a word of English."

Hesitantly Maryetta joined the others. Standing with her hands behind her she found herself facing the tall American. He took her small hand in his and asked her name.

"I am Maryetta—from America," she added.

Instantly he was interested. "You seem young to be studying in Europe."

"Well, you see, *monsieur*, I live here in Brussels. I have been here for years. Oh, but *monsieur*—never have I heard such artistry! How do I thank you properly? But—here—" and she removed the rose from her dress and handed it to him.

"You speak English with an accent," he said.

"The years here, sir. I have learned to speak as the people do, but I do not forget my own tongue."

"When will you return to your own country?"

"That I do not know."

Maryetta's countenance saddened so suddenly that she stirred instant sympathy in the sensitive artist. He waited politely for an explanation.

"My father has forgotten me," she explained.

"No father could forget a child like you. Tell me, is there anything I might do for you?"

"I think—you might pray. Would you do that?" Her words were spoken with little hope.

He hesitated a moment and then replied, "*Mademoiselle*, indeed I shall keep your rose, and every time I look at it I promise you I shall pray for you."

He was then on to the next in line, leaving Maryetta ecstatic. The music—the honor—the promise lifting her into a never-never land!

Walking home with Sister Josephine, she now felt that the street-corner music profaned the perfect evening, insulting the magic and the aura of the music she had just heard—the music of the masters, music that clung and wound its beauty around the heart.

It was only when she climbed the stairs to the sleeping convent and stepped inside the great door that she felt the mood change. It was always quiet here at night, but there was now an unnatural silence, portentous and foreboding.

Entering her room, she noticed that Janine had left a candle burning for her. She undressed and shook off the unwelcome gloom and got into bed. Lying there, she let her thoughts wander back to the concert hall and the handsome American. Music began to permeate her thoughts, lulling her into a blissful euphoria.

It was with a start that she became aware of a shadowy figure standing by her bed.

"Janine, is that you?"

"Yes, Marie."

"Why are you not in bed and asleep?"

"Oh, Marie, I cannot sleep. I am certain our Sister Celeste is very ill. Her temperature went up right after you left—dreadfully high. Mother Dominique has been with her all evening."

Instantly Maryetta was on her feet and wrapping a shawl around her slim shoulders. Janine started to follow.

"No, Janine. It is best I go alone. When I come back I will tell you how she is."

Reluctantly Janine complied.

Down the long gallery and under the flickering candlelight Maryetta hurried. She tapped gently on Sister Celeste's door. Receiving no response, she pushed it open and let herself in, quickly closing the door behind her.

There on the narrow bed lay her beloved sister. A candle burned low on the table where they had first shared their Christmas bread, the wavering, feeble light lending a ghastly pallor to the nun's features.

A gripping fear took hold of Maryetta's pounding heart. "Sister Celeste?"

It was no more than whisper, but Sister Celeste stirred.

"Sister, it is I—Marie."

The nun turned troubled eyes in Maryetta's direction. "Did you like your concert, dear?"

"I did not come about the concert. I just learned that you are very ill."

"Yes, dear—" Then she was quiet.

Maryetta held the nun's hand and then touched her forehead.

"You are dreadfully hot. Let me sponge you down."

"Oh—would you?"

Maryetta left the room and returned with a basin of water. "Sister—you frighten me."

"Yes, I am a little frightened too—" but the response was cut short as Sister Celeste wretched violently. "Do not—call—the—Reverend Mother. She has been with me all evening. I'll soon be all right."

"Oh, Sister, you are not all right. I must get help for you!"

The nun lifted a protesting hand.

"I must disobey you . . . forgive me . . ." and Maryetta fled the room, heading directly for the Prioress.

Waking an anxious Mother Dominique, Maryetta followed her back through the corridors and stood silently watching as the Mother ministered to the nun.

"I believe she will rest now, Marie. Thank you for calling me. Go back to bed and pray for her. If she is not better by morning, I shall call in a physician."

Maryetta hesitated, unwilling to leave her friend, but the order had been given.

Janine was waiting for her when she returned.

"How is she, Marie?" she asked.

"She is resting now, though I found her very ill."

"Oh, Marie—if anything happens to Sister Celeste, whatever would we do? I think I should run away or—just die myself!"

The impassioned remark, like a wind in dry leaves, sent Maryetta's thoughts into turmoil.

"Go to bed, Janine!"

"As you please—but first I shall pray!"

Once again anger swept over Maryetta, resentment stripping away her tenuous desire to believe and to trust the unseen God. Why Sister Celeste, the loveliest soul in all of Christendom? Why should a saint like the gentle Celeste have to suffer? Why not the insidious Anunciata?

Janine knelt beside her bed, holding her prayer beads. Her eyes solemn with reproach, she questioned Maryetta.

"Why, Marie, do you not pray?"

Maryetta did not like the question.

"I am different from you, Janine. You Catholics are taught to pray just as you are taught to wash your face or brush your hair. It is natural for you. I do not feel right about praying to the saints!"

"But they can help!"

"I know you believe that, Janine, but it is not enough for me. I cannot explain it." She turned away from her clearly disappointed friend and climbed into bed.

9

THE NIGHT PASSED AND BY MORNING SISTER CELESTE SEEMED TO rally. For two days Maryetta made it a ritual to steal away from the breakfast hour and visit her friend. It was not easy, for her schedule was demanding and she had duties she could not neglect.

She entered the room while it was early. Shadows were moving on the inside walls and except for an occasional breath of wind the outside trees were still and silent.

"Sister?"

The nun stirred and turned toward Maryetta, her face ashen and her eyes enormous with deep shadows beneath. She managed a wan smile.

"I have been looking for you. How many days has it been?" Sister Celeste asked.

She looked strange without the soft folds of the veil and the clean white wimple. Short-cropped blond curls lay damp against her temples. Her features were so delicate—Maryetta could see that she must have been a striking beauty in her youth.

She reached a hand toward Maryetta, who was quick to grasp it.

"You have not told me about the concert. I wanted so to hear."

"You are much too ill."

"Please!"

Maryetta picked up a silver-backed brush and began to smooth Sister Celeste's hair.

"There now. I will get you water to drink."

"My dear, don't go. I am not thirsty—nor hungry. Just talk to me."

Satisfied that Sister Celeste wanted company more than anything else, Maryetta pulled a chair close beside the bed and described her night at the concert. She went into detail about the audience, the fashionable clothing, the Alexandrian styles, the chignon hairdressing, the lavish jewelry, and the beautiful music hall interior.

"And the music . . . Tell me, was Jerome Cavell all that the critics have said?"

"Oh, yes, and more—such a fine gentleman. You can never guess what he did at the end."

"Tell me!"

"He invited all second-year students to come to the platform—and he shook hands with me! And oh, sister, if you had not given me the rose!"

"The rose?"

"I gave it to him, and he promised to keep it—and—and every time he looks at it he will say a prayer for me."

"I am rewarded!" said Celeste, her face brightening, sending warmth where only moments ago there had been dark shadows.

"He is such a great man, I am sure God will hear him."

"My Maryetta, when will you learn that our God is not influenced by kingly personages or peasant rags? It is the heart that matters."

And then she was quiet, making Maryetta wonder if the conversation had been too taxing.

"Sister?"

Celeste opened her eyes and looked past Maryetta. "I have a strange feeling that you will see Jerome Cavell again," she stated.

"That would be impossible. He goes on to Paris and Rome and then back to his own country."

"You will see and you will know that every hard thing in this life has a purpose—a preparation for something good somewhere in our lifetime—unless we choke it out with the weeds of self-pity or bitterness."

Having said this, she closed her eyes, dismissing Maryetta. She lapsed quickly into an exhausted sleep. Maryetta tucked her covers close to her chin, planted a kiss on her forehead, and left.

The day moved on at its usual rapid pace, and Maryetta was able only once to look in on Sister Celeste. As it was evident that the sister was sleeping, Maryetta decided herself to retire.

THE OBSTREPEROUS MORNING bell awoke and summoned Maryetta to a new day. She must make a hurried visit to Sister Celeste's room, but of course she must first brush the hair of the young girls and see they were dressed properly. She pressed them into action, dismissed them, and hurried toward the nun's room.

As she neared her small chamber she could see two of the sisters standing like sentinels before the door. She recognized Sister Josephine and Sister Anunciata. They were whispering and looking directly at her.

"I came to look in on Sister Celeste."

"Why are you not at breakfast?" asked Sister Anunciata.

Maryetta stammered out an excuse and moved toward the door, but Sister Josephine stepped in her path.

"No, Marie! The doctor is with Sister now. Mother Dominique sent for him early this morning."

The frightened animal look came back in Maryetta's eyes. She looked from one to the other and back at the slightly ajar door—then heard the doctor's muffled exclamation.

"Cieux de misericorde—c'est le typhoide!"

Open-mouthed, the nuns stared at one another. Maryetta stood shocked and pale.

"Please—did I hear right?" she asked. "Does Sister Celeste have the typhoid?"

"Marie! Go directly to breakfast and repeat nothing you have heard. Go!"

Maryetta turned, stumbling and trembling, and hurried toward the dining room. If the Sister had typhoid, the entire convent would come under quarantine. Even worse, Maryetta would be barred from the nun's presence. The memory of the wooden barrier at her mother's door stirred terror, as Maryetta recalled how it had brought an end forever to her mother's smile and her mother's arms around her. Surely—oh, surely she would not be kept from her one true friend!

Hours passed, the longest of Maryetta's life, and an air of gloom settled in. Strips of cloth were nailed across Sister Celeste's door and word spread through the convent that no one was to go near the contaminated room without special permission. The good Mother gathered the children together and explained the seriousness of the disease, but Maryetta listened sullenly. If the sister were that sick, surely she would need human contact. She held back while the others filed out of the room, then approached the Prioress.

"Mother Dominique, I should like to serve Sister Celeste—feed her—bathe her—please."

The old nun looked at the slim American with the solemn gray eyes, so earnestly pleading. She had not realized that Maryetta had matured so fast, nor that she had such a frail appearance. Except for the rounding face, she was indeed very slight. Her innocence touched the heart of the Prioress. It was difficult to deny her the request; yet she could see that the young girl was not up to the work Celeste's care would demand.

"I commend you, Marie, for your unselfishness, but you are much too young. The task will require someone stronger and more experienced."

"Oh, please, Mother! I must help her!"

"I wish I might grant your request, dear, but there are so many things that I must consider. I cannot risk even one of you children getting typhoid. I am the responsible one, you know."

"My family would never care. You must know that. I know you know that!"

The older woman waxed more emphatic.

"I am sorry, Marie. I cannot accept your offer. Go along to your classes, and I will keep you informed of Sister Celeste's condition."

The refusal seared like a branding iron and Maryetta turned away, defeated and resenting afresh the subservient role she was forced always to play. Why must she always be at the mercy of unfeeling people? Would the day ever come when she could make her own decisions?

Days moved on, and Mother Dominique kept her word. Maryetta found a note each day on her commode telling her of Sister Celeste's condition. She was suffering through the worst of it, the most traumatic period of the illness; shifting temperatures, tremors, and exhaustion. The disturbing reports made sleep impossible for Maryetta. Half knowledge and vague rumors mixed with fear were torturous.

Unable one night to stand the uncertainty any longer, Maryetta flung her gray blankets off and, wrapping herself in her old shawl, slipped out into the dark corridor. Only pale candlelight sent flickering shadows upon the walls. She moved with the stealth of a cat, running from one of the concave *intrados* to another, stopping, peering with animal-like caution, listening for footsteps or the rustle of coarse kersey. Arriving at Celeste's room, she first pressed an ear to the heavy door. Satisfied that no attendant was inside, she untied the despised strips of cloth and slipped inside.

Despite the gray of her face, Sister Celeste was clearly breathing.

Maryetta whispered her name.

"Go away, child—go away—"

"I can't do that, sister. I came to help."

"No one can help me, Marie—and you endanger yourself. Please go!"

"You shiver! I can't leave until I put more covers on you."

Too weak for further protest, the nun submitted to the loving hands.

"I love you, sister, and I must help you. Tell me, is there

anything you would have me do?"

The nun's answer was slow in coming, but with great effort she spoke. "The drawer—top—letter. Post to my brother."

Maryetta opened the designated drawer, retrieved the addressed envelope and tucked it in her clothing. This done, she went for water, returned to Celeste's bedside and began to sponge the invalid.

"What are these red marks, sister?" she asked. Then realizing how difficult it was for her to talk, she added quickly, "Never mind. You must not talk. Just rest."

Having bathed the nun, Maryetta pulled a chair beside the bed and reached for her hand. Hours ticked away and Maryetta began to doze. Suddenly she felt her patient stiffen.

"What is it, sister?" she asked, fully awake.

"Marie, you must go—I think I am dying."

"Oh, sister, you must not die—I shall have no one!"

"Pray, Maryetta—forgive—"

The sound of her own name brought a rush of tears. "I'm not good at that—but for you—"

"No—not for me—for others—for yourself—"

"Yes—sister."

"And do not grieve for me—please. If my brother does not come, promise me you will see that I return to Mechelen. Bury me near the church where the carillons play—please—do that."

Maryetta was sure the sister's mind had taken flight—gone to the ridiculous—to the past—perhaps to treasured memories. And why, Maryetta wondered, did dying people ask for the impossible? How could she possibly keep from grieving if Sister Celeste died? And how could she possibly see to a burial?

"Now go, Marie—trouble for you—here."

In exasperation Maryetta answered, "Sister, if I were to spend eternity in hell, I could not leave you to die alone!"

Her words were strong with conviction. To be certain that her beloved friend understood, she climbed onto the bed, settled down beside her, and placed her arms around her.

"Rest, sister. I am not leaving."

Sister Celeste relaxed against Maryetta and stopped her protesting, and the night moved on.

When dawn broke, Maryetta awoke to the shocked expressions of three nuns peering down at her. They were aghast at their discovery, but not too shocked to ask questions!

"Were you not forbidden?" "Foolish girl—were you not told to stay away? You will be punished!"

Stunned, Maryetta turned to look into the face of Sister Celeste and saw that her friend had passed through the deep waters and moved into the light of heaven.

"Oh, no—no—no!" she cried, sobs breaking forth and wracking her slim frame.

She could feel the nuns extricating her fingers. Breaking her grasp, two of them pulled her to her feet and dragged her to her own room, where they closed the door angrily and left her alone in the frozen stupor of grief.

Suddenly the halls were alive with activity, garbled voices, and the sound of running feet. Maryetta walked into the long closet where the girls' coats were hung.

"You will remain in your room for the day," Sister Josephine had said. "You also must dress."

Her clothing had been placed on her bed, and the nun had left with the administrative invective still ringing in Maryetta's ears. "I shall be back in an hour!"

Janine came in almost as soon as Sister Josephine had left, and found Maryetta crumpled on the closet floor, still in her night clothes.

"I waited for you, Maryetta. I waited for you all night. I had to know. Is it true that Sister Celeste is dead?"

Maryetta looked at Janine with unseeing eyes, her brows wrinkled and her expression blank.

"Come—you must dress or they'll be angry."

The fear of reprisal drove the gentle Janine to move with

unnatural speed. She managed to get clothes on Maryetta. It was not easy, for Maryetta was definitely in a trance.

An envelope fell from her clothing, and Janine picked it up.

"What is this?"

Maryetta scowled and tried to remember. The long, fearful night—ah, yes, the promise—the ridiculous promise.

"Mail it, Janine. Mail it right away."

Janine placed the letter in her pocket. "I have to go."

Maryetta nodded and sank back upon the bed expressionless.

"Why, God—why don't I feel something—anything but this—nothing? Living is nothing—nothing. Why can't I die—die with Sister Celeste?"

SISTER JOSEPHINE RETURNED WITH a softer expression on her features. She knew that Maryetta was not deserving of punishment, that the young girl's inner suffering was enough. Peering around furtively, she removed a sandwich from the folds of her skirt and placed it on the pillow.

"Eat," she ordered, and this time her voice exuded sympathy.

No one else came for the rest of the day. When evening arrived, Sister Josephine returned and was clearly disappointed to find the sandwich untouched. In the evening Maryetta's friends came, each with a loving touch of empathy and eyes red from tears. Both Antoinette and Janine hung close by, hoping Maryetta would feel their concern. Louise wept openly through the night.

This went on for two days until Mother Dominique summoned Maryetta to her office.

"I am sorry, Marie, that I felt obliged to punish you. You did disobey me, you know. Now that is all past. Go to the kitchen and get some food, then go your classes. Do you understand?"

Maryetta nodded silently.

"You are dismissed."

Within a day's time a very handsome middle-aged man came to see the Prioress. One of the girls overhead him say that he planned to lay the remains of his sister in a small churchyard near the carillons. Maryetta felt relieved to know that she had served her beloved friend and that Sister Celeste's dying wish would be granted. How good it was that the nun had someone who cared.

She wondered wistfully if there would be anyone to care if she herself were to die. Would she be buried on foreign soil—forgotten with the last shovel full of earth?

She returned to her classes, a dull ache in her heart. Plagued by grief and riddled with questions, she went through the motions expected of her, finding her only relief in the few hours she slept. Every waking moment brought back the pain of her loss.

She questioned the God she had hoped to trust and went on feeling the loneliness and the buffeting of adverse winds. Who was this one who rode upon the heavens? The one Nigel Edmunds had said was her help, her refuge, who would thrust out her enemies before her . . . where was this God?

But her cup of suffering was not yet full, and this God would yet take her where she would not choose to go.

A WEEK PASSED, AND several of the girls complained of persistent headaches—not a passing inconvenience, but a throbbing, sickly head pain. Then it was Maryetta's turn. The Prioress showed great alarm when the nosebleeds started and all the symptoms pointed to the same illness that had claimed the life of Sister Celeste.

Alert to a possible siege, the Mother set the nuns to clearing out large supply rooms and hauling in enough cots to accommodate the students who were growing worse. By the time a week had passed, over half the students had come down with typhoid. News filtered in from the outside that not only had the city come under attack, but an epidemic was sweeping the country.

Into the depths of physical anguish Maryetta now sank. She had said she would spend eternity in hell before letting Sister Celeste die alone—and she was certain she had predicted her own fate. She passed in and out of consciousness, shivered with the cold, sweltered in the heat of fever, and shook violently with the tremors.

In one of her conscious moments she was aware of swift-moving hands administering cool water to her flaming body, someone brushing her hair with the gentleness of an angel and demanding, too, that she swallow something bitter. She recognized Sister Anunciata! Dizzily she thought she must truly be delirious. In anguish she cried for God to take her out of her misery, to take her to be with Sister Celeste and her own mother.

But that was not in the plan of God. One morning she awoke—weak, but definitely over the ordeal.

She looked around the room at the dozens of cots of sick children. Seeing neither Janine, Antoinette, nor Louise, she entered into the torment of fear. A busy nun assured her that all three of those girls had survived, but soberly continued that Clarice and Isobel had not.

The news stunned her. Why had she, of all people, survived?

"The old ones—the nuns in the garret?" she asked.

"They are fine. Not one has come down with typhoid!" answered the nun.

"That must be a miracle!" said Maryetta.

"Perhaps. But then, they live an isolated life."

"They live a life close to God!" said Maryetta, feeling her own shortcomings.

Antoinette sent her jeweled mirror to let Maryetta know she had learned of her recovery. It was a generous gesture, and Maryetta was able to smile some as she raised it to her face.

Then came the anguished cry!

"*Dieu de Misericorde!* What has happened to my hair?"

Maryetta reached up a frail hand and touched what remained of her thick, light brown hair.

"*Mes cheveux—qu'est-ce-qui s'est passé à mes cheveux?*"

"Quiet, Marie! You will trouble the sick! It is enough that you are alive. Be thankful!" It was Sister Anunciata, weary and over-worked, who had so chided.

There had been no time to see to the care of hair with much more important needs pressing. Together Sister Josephine and Sister Anunciata had decided that they would not wrestle with snarled hair, but would cut it off. Hair could grow again.

Maryetta remembered how Sister Celeste had said that it takes all kinds to make a world. Sister Anunciata was living proof of that comment—a strange kind of person—a mixture of harshness with a measure of compassion as well as a zeal for good works, and this time Maryetta felt no resentment toward the inconsistency of the woman.

Eventually the pale horse of pestilence rode on and life began to resume its old order. Mourning gave way to a solemn acceptance, and the traumatic days passed away.

Maryetta discovered that she could go on, even without the saintly Celeste. But the new tragedy awakened again her hostility toward her stepmother. One day she would go to that evil woman and tell her how vicious she was—how cruel and deserving of retribution.

Now, without the searching eyes of Sister Celeste, Maryetta felt she could secretly cosset her bitterness . . . and go on planning for her day of revenge.

10

It was the end of 1868 and the world was growing smaller. Cyrus Field had at long last succeeded in laying the Atlantic cable, and communication between the old continent and the new America had become a permanent reality. Now news could travel faster under water than it ever had by surface.

The new States were sending colorful accounts of wide western expansion, of cattle drives, Indian wars, gold and silver mines. Tales of realized hopes for men hardy enough to work new soil were enticing adventurous Easterners in America to quit their farms and to go west in increased numbers. Fields of iron were discovered on Lake Superior's northern boundary, and railroads reached long tentacles beyond the Mississippi.

The Scot, English, and the Hollander were investing dollars and time in the new country, and names like Carnegie and Studebaker were on the tongues of European investors. The comely Alexandra had presented Britain's Prince Edward with two sons, the younger more personable than the older. Now the young mother was expecting her third child, sparking avid interest in the gossip of plebeian circles. In the Netherlands, Willem III was worrying his Counselors for fear there would be no reigning heir after his demise, and Belgium's Leopold II was spending most of his time on the French Riviera.

Maryetta, now sixteen, had settled in to the quiet life of the convent school. Her hair had grown again, though with a reluctance that brought it only to her shoulders, Typhoid, it seemed, had been very ungracious to those girls who had survived the dreadful scourge. Still, with feminine persistence they learned to coax their locks into presentable styles—upswept, for the most part. They teased the ends into coarse curls and enjoyed renewed interest in their appearance.

For Maryetta there were now more responsibilities. Along with the care of specific children and a limited number of students in French, she entered classes in European culinary skills. She had begun to realize that her future depended on herself and that any change in her life would have to come from her own energy and abilities.

The reticence and the reserve of the past were gone, and she applied herself to her studies with the gusto of a young Hercules raising the Pillars of Abyla. She would build her own world, one that no one could take from her. With the new goal and fresh determination, she found solace in her books. In no time, the goal became an obsession.

BY JUNE OF 1869, final examinations were on the horizon, and Maryetta's intention to surpass her peers, to garner for herself every honor offered—including the gold watch presented each outstanding student—was all that filled her mind.

Most of the other girls were content to be receiving creditable grades—most, that is, with the exception of Florence Charmay. The sparring between Maryetta and Florence had begun in earnest during the last few months of the school year. By graduation day they were scarcely speaking to one another.

Over fifty students filed into the small assembly room and sat stiffly awaiting the results. As usual, the affable Janine was at Maryetta's side, sitting as close to her friend as she possibly could. She was by far the more nervous of the two. She leaned close to whisper, "One more year, Maryetta. One more year and we shall go home for good!"

"Shhhh." Maryetta was not interested in anything beyond the present moment. What was on the paper the Prioress held in her hands? Did it hold any promise for her future? Either Maryetta would go on to freedom or be forever defeated. If she failed here to attain her goal she would have to accept her lonely life—forget her home, her father, and everything she wanted most. She kept her eyes riveted on the broad-faced nun, hoping to see some evidence of partiality.

It seemed that the 'Ave Marias' the young novitiates were singing would never end. The long prayers and encomiums dragged on, and then the certificates of promotion were passed out. Everything seeming unnecessarily drawn out.

Then the Mother took her place at the podium, in her hands the coveted gold locket watch. It dangled there, brilliantly reflecting the lamplight.

Janine, still bug-eyed, pressed close to Maryetta, her heart pounding. Would the good Mother never get on?

"It gives me great pleasure to bestow this award upon a young lady who came to us as a small child."

Had not most of them come as small children?

The Prioress went on. "She has not only attained the highest scholastic honors, but we have been privileged to watch her grow into a responsible and lovely young woman."

Maryetta's thoughts grew uncharitable. That could not possibly be Florence Charmay.

"Marie Corbay—will you please come forward?"

Stunned for a fleeting moment, Maryetta sat fixed. The blow—the blow that broke the everlasting shackles—and lightning breaking the bonds—and it was real!

It was Janine's voice that penetrated Maryetta's thoughts.

"Maryetta—oh, Maryetta! I think I shall faint!"

Janine had paled so that Maryetta hesitated to leave her. Then she grinned—laughed aloud—or was it relief finding expression! Ah, now she would soar—and no one would hold her!

In the habit of obeying, Maryetta got to her feet. In an aura of overwhelming joy she ascended the platform. Trembling, she was only half aware of the gold chain being slipped over her head. Of course she would not touch it until she was alone—but, oh, the feeling of it against her breast!

The Mother kissed her affectionately on both cheeks and dismissed her. Walking back to her chair, Maryetta looked full into the face of her rival. She had expected chagrin, but not the flaming hatred she saw there.

A wave of sympathy for Florence swept over Maryetta. Surely her anger would not last. There had to be losers where there was a contest, and surely they had both considered that before they had launched out into the rivalry. . . .

Janine left the following day for her summer vacation. She departed in a lithesome state of mind, knowing that her dearest friend had won the honors for which she had labored so hard and so long.

And Maryetta? She could slow down, work at a slower pace and look forward with a buoyant knowledge that when fall came she would be in her final days at the convent. Her long night would be over and her future free from arbitrators!

The summer days of 1869 passed quickly and quietly, with Florence continuing to ignore Maryetta. Then the girls were returning with vivid accounts of their family reunions. Market days were now an even greater treat, for Janine was allowed to accompany Maryetta on these excursions. They could at leisure enjoy the sights of the city, but it was not the sights of the city that piqued Maryetta's curiosity. There was a new radiance in the dark eyes of Janine, and Maryetta suspected that an announcement would be soon forthcoming.

"I have met someone, Marie," she confided.

Maryetta studied her friend. Janine was beautiful—her complexion flawless, cheeks olive-toned and generously brushed with rose, hair as black as a raven's wing and rebelliously curly in spite of the restraints, her motions graceful and her spirit luminously bright.

"I am surprised it has taken so long," said Maryetta facetiously.

"I met him at the park by the Linkeroever. It was very accidental."

"—and you fell in love at first sight."

Janine laughed, showing even white teeth. "Well, almost. I saw him afterward—often. He is an accountant at a diamond bourse—and he wants to marry me."

Maryetta laughed happily with her friend, seriously doubting that anyone could fall in love so quickly.

"I am happy for you, Janine," she said.

Letters came almost every day for Janine, and Maryetta sensed that her dear friend was moving away into a new world. Even though they would have their moments of sharing, Maryetta knew she would soon experience again the loneliness that so plagued her life.

"What is it like to have a man kiss you?" Maryetta dared to ask. "He did kiss you, didn't he?"

Janine's face went rapturous—and turned crimson.

"That is hard to describe, Marie. A man's love lifts you out of the millions and makes you feel you are the only person in the world. And his kiss? That's a new dimension—Roman candles and sparklers all at once—like putting the last piece of a puzzle together—home for the flying pigeon—Mercy! Did I say all that?" And she clamped her hand over her mouth, though her eyes sparkled with laughter.

"And how did he propose?"

"Oh . . . violins . . . a restaurant dinner . . . flowers . . . and diamonds . . . all like a dream."

Maryetta became quiet—thoughtful—then spoke with longing.

"I have dreamed of having someone like that—but of course I never shall. Look at me! Always struggling to hide my ruined hair. A man would notice that and think me deceitful. I hate deceit!"

Janine faced her friend, her eyes tender and loving.

"My dearest Marie, truly you do not know how beautiful you are. One does not see little imperfections where there is so much inner beauty. It radiates from you—all kindness and love. I am certain that someday a man of quality and perception will see all that I see, what you try to hide."

And with an impulsive kiss, the small Walloon girl was gone. Wistfully Maryetta watched her leave, knowing that their days together at the convent were numbered. By the time June and graduation came around again, their shared memories would be all either could sequester in her heart. Sadness moved in—and Maryetta wondered why it was that the truly precious things of life were so transitory.

It was Sister Josephine who came with the letter. As Maryetta looked at her, she realized that the nun was beginning to age. Fine lines had etched themselves into her face. Even her eyes were a little dim. Maryetta wondered if the Sister would join the old ones in the garret and spend her last years making lace.

The nun placed the envelope in Maryetta's hands and smiled warmly. Maryetta looked it over hopefully, wanting desperately to see that it had come from California, but there was no such evidence. Instead it bore a New England address—far removed from the golden state on the Pacific. She opened it and read the straight-to-the-point contents:

November 5, 1869
My dear granddaughter,

It has only recently come to my attention that you have been abroad now for the past nine years. I did not keep in touch with your father after your mother died and he married another.

His new wife has written me of your whereabouts and offered me money if I would take you to live with me. The money I declined in no uncertain terms. I do not appreciate her attitude. She says that your father is much too busy establishing sanitariums to be encumbered with a family. Seems he should have thought of that before he had one. I have written to tell her so, and to inform her that I am offering a home to you where nothing will be put ahead of caring for one's own flesh and blood.

Your mother was my only child, and I was not in favor of having her go to the West where savages and bad weather would have to be faced. I now wish to help you all I can, so I am inviting you to come and live with me and my wife. We would really like to have you. Trudy is my second wife and a good, kind woman. I, myself, am only a simple cabinet maker and our ways are not highfalutin—but we are comfortable.

Your stepmother sent your fare, so I am enclosing it. Let me know immediately, please, if and when you are to arrive, so I can meet you properly. You must book passage to the Newburyport, Massachusetts station.

Your Grandfather,
Nathan Downing

Sister Josephine stood observing and questioning, and Maryetta returned a blank stare.

"Is it bad news?" asked the sister.

"No, sister. It seems to be a grandfather I have never met. He has invited me to come and live with him."

"Where?"

"In America." Maryetta looked at the round scrawl on the envelope. "In a place called Byfield, Massachusetts."

"This grandfather—do you know him?"

"I think my mother spoke of him—but it was so long ago. I know next to nothing of my mother's family. He sounds kind."

For a long time afterward, the letter stirred new fires of bitterness toward the selfish Lydia and rancor and disenchantment toward a father who did not keep his promises. But here, it seemed, was the only relative who seemed to care, and Maryetta felt her heart warming toward the grandfather who had written.

One day Sister Josephine asked her if she had made a decision concerning his offer.

"I do not know, Sister. It would be nice to have a family."

Sister Josephine patted Maryetta's hand. Such things as these Maryetta would miss—the quiet gentleness of the nuns—the sound of the heavy woven skirts as the sisters went about their duties—yes, many things. This life was really all that Maryetta had known. What could the outside possibly be like?

THE LAST MONTHS OF school passed swiftly. The winter months were soon over, and spring made her balmy debut. The chestnuts were in bloom—some red, some white—and parks took on their pale and vibrant shades of green, as well as sending forth the fragrance of watered earth. It all brought forth a decided restlessness that Maryetta could not dispel. Graduation would be over in a matter of days—and then what?

11

THE DAY AFTER GRADUATION, MARYETTA RECEIVED A SUMMONS to the office of the Prioress.

"You are now well qualified, Marie, for a position of trust, possibly that of a governess. I am sure you shall have no problem finding a good situation should you choose to remain in Europe. Your father has paid his final obligation, and you are free to leave."

"How much time do I have, Mother Dominique?" asked Maryetta, hiding again the hurt she was feeling that her father could not have written her.

"I believe one month should be time enough."

Antoinette, Louise, and Janine wept unashamedly. Even though they were, each one, pleased to be starting a new phase of their own lives, the shared experiences of ten years had bonded them, and the parting was excruciatingly painful.

With her comrades gone to their own homes and only a few students left at the school for the summer, the convent after mid-June became painfully silent, like an echoing dark labyrinth.

One ray of sunshine came during the tarrying days in the form of an invitation to the wedding of Janine Turgot and Pierre Larousse. The nuns, too, had received invitations, so it was with enthusiasm that they made plans to travel together to Antwerp. They boarded a train that took them through Mechelen, where each of the travelers bowed her head and said a prayer for their beloved Celeste.

On into the beautiful countryside, past the five-acre farms and market gardens, by St. Rombout's Tower and close to the sweet-sounding carillons and Rubens's city, the lovely Patrician homes, the ancient chapels and past the *Koninklijk Museum voor Schöne Kunsten*, the Breweries, the Butchers' Guild Hall, and on to Saint Charles.

There the wedding took place in the solemn setting of Quellin statuary and artistic paintings. Janine, in heirloom Valencienne lace, was never more beautiful. Her joy had brought a radiance to her shining dark eyes as she joined heart and hand with her "prince." Pierre was everything Maryetta had envisioned—tall, handsome, and thoroughly captivated by the charming Janine.

The festivities that followed the high mass allowed Maryetta only a brief opportunity to bid her friend a final good-bye.

"I have decided to go home, Janine—home to America. Here is my future address in the States. Please write to me."

Good-bye so lightly said—so deeply felt—and then Maryetta returned to the convent with the nuns. Now she moved seriously to be about her packing and securing passage to America. There were letters to write: one to Ellen and one to her grandfather.

An answer came promptly from Ellen, agreeing to meet Maryetta when she arrived in New York. Maryetta wondered if they would recognize one another—how much had the ten-year separation changed them both?—but the thought of actually seeing her beloved nurse came with joyful anticipation.

Coach travel would be the least costly, so she arranged her overnight posts in Belgium and would do that nightly in Britain. She remembered how the social-conscious Lydia had overpacked for her stint in London. Maryetta would not make that mistake. She owned very little, so one good-sized valise would do.

Into the valise went the white gloves she had worn to Jerome Cavell's concert and Janine's wedding, followed by a careful packing of things she treasured: her watercolors and her oils, the magenta-colored covered history notebook so well done in calligraphy—its record of Europe's kings and popes so diligently copied. Hardly the thing that would interest her Presbyterian grandfather; still—someday, perhaps, someone would value it.

Since it was summer, she would require very few articles of clothing—blouses, skirts, toiletries, and underwear, a light *paletot* and a few scarves. She would wear her narrow-brimmed hat and travel gloves. Doubtless, her clothing would mark her as European bourgeoisie, but of that she cared little. She was going home to her own country, where folk were valued for character and not for their titles.

She looked at her gold watch—the golden token that promised so much. Winning it had confirmed for her that her abilities could triumph over adversity and injustice. She held it until it became warm in her hands and felt some sadness, for owning it had estranged her from Florence. How could something inanimate have the power to alienate?

Sister Celeste had said she should pray for those who hated her—but why should Florence hate her? The contest had been a fair one! Sister Celeste had asked too much. The maxim may have been right for the departed sister, for she had never been the object of anyone's hate.

Still, the words of the sister would not go away. They seemed branded into Maryetta's heart. "Do good, not evil to those who bear you ill will."

Could she really leave the convent having failed her beloved Sister Celeste? The question persisted and robbed Maryetta both of peace and sleep. That night in desperation Maryetta unclasped the chain and, with the locket watch in hand, made her way to Florence's room.

Florence had chosen to remain at the convent and enter the order, though Maryetta was convinced that God would have to work a miracle to mellow Florence's disposition. Perhaps that was what convents were for!

When Maryetta knocked on the door, Florence called out for her to enter. Facing her antagonist, Maryetta stammered miserably.

"I—I—have come to say good-bye—and to wish you well as you begin your novitiate."

Florence stared, unbelief and distrust clouding her dark features.

"I am sorry we have not been friends, Florence. I really am. When I won the honors and the watch I was not trying to better you. I was trying to prove something to myself—something I had to know. Please try to understand."

There was still no response, so Maryetta reached for Florence's hand. Placing the watch there, she folded the other girl's fingers down over it.

Florence pulled away.

"No! I want you to have it. You worked hard for it—that I well know!"

Florence softened, the brightness of the gold reflecting in her face. "I don't know—" she managed.

"I am going back to America. I leave from the Central Road Coach station at the Royal Inn at six o'clock tomorrow morning. I need your prayers; the journey will be long, and you know how little I have traveled. I am really a little frightened."

Maryetta left then, with Florence still holding the watch and frowning.

Maryetta slept more soundly that night than she had for a long time and was up before the sun rose still wondering about her decision to return to America. To leave Belgium . . . the familiar sounds and scenes of the marketplace, horses' hooves on Belgian blocks, the picturesque bridges, gothic structures, the cathedrals. It was much to contemplate.

She went early to the inn, where she had to wait until four monstrous horses were hitched to an English coach. The wait gave her time to gather her wits and eat the orange she had purchased at the market.

Saying farewell to familiar things had not been easy. Saying good-bye to the only parent she had known for ten years, wiping away Mother Dominique's tears and her own. Preparing to board, she watched as others bade farewell to family members. Now she was truly alone, without so much as a distant relative to wish her Godspeed. Loneliness crowded in, chilling her, and she looked up the street with a forlorn expression on her face.

It was then that she saw the familiar garb of the sisterhood and recognized the inscrutable features of Florence Charmay.

"I came to wish you journeying mercies," said Florence with some embarrassment.

"Oh, Florence!"

It was all Maryetta could say, and the girls were suddenly in each other's arms.

"Truly, Maryetta. I could not sleep all night thinking about you. When I got up this morning and found you had already left, I felt terrible. I knew I could never keep your watch! Here, take it. It is indeed yours. Think kindly of me when you look at it. You should treasure it."

Maryetta was astounded. "You really mean that?"

"Oh, yes. I hurried here, praying you had not left."

Maryetta took the watch, knowing it was better for Florence to give it up than it was for herself and rejoicing inwardly that Florence was willing.

The footman stacked suitcases and small traveling trunks atop the coach, and the horses strained to be off. Maryetta kissed Florence and boarded the coach. Leaning from the window, she called to her friend.

"Florence! As soon as I am able, I'll send you a teapot. Invite the new little ones to your room for tea!"

For a moment Florence looked perplexed; then a light spread over the serious features, and Florence Charmay smiled and nodded!

OUT OF THE CITY, pitching and rolling, rode Maryetta Cobbet on the first mile of her long journey. Her traveling companions included one overbearing man who claimed most of the seating space and deemed it his duty to order the coachman about like an overzealous feudal lord; a dowdy, overdressed woman opposite; and beside her a small, fragile-looking white-haired man with a large nose and heavy-lidded intelligent brown eyes. He studied Maryetta, then turned his attention to a paper he was holding.

They had not gone far when the autocrat insisted on closing all of the windows, which brought Maryetta discomfort and a headache.

The white-haired man could see that she was miserable and made an effort to help her. In excellent French he said, "Sir, I find it very unreasonable that the windows remain closed. The young lady needs both air and enough of the seat for which she has paid. You should be gentleman enough to show her some consideration."

The obnoxious traveler drew himself up haughtily and proceeded to ignore the speaker, whereupon the little man took it upon himself to open a window, deeply ingratiating himself to the shy Maryetta.

"Thank you, sir. I did not get your name," she said.

"Solomon Levi," he answered.

Maryetta marveled that the kindness had come from a Jew. She had heard so often that the Jew was concerned only with his own interests. Why, she wondered, should any one particular people have engendered such bias? Remembering the history she'd studied of the Inquisition, she could readily see how the unfortunate Jew might develop a hard-shelled interest in his right to survive. That had also been her choice, and she felt an empathy for the Israelite and all of his people.

The rest of the journey was as uneventful as it was wearisome. Her destination seemed far away, and she missed her convent bed.

Maryetta was only too glad to arrive at the ferry. The air was a little oily, but nevertheless cool. She went on board with the passengers, and the ferry pulled away from the quay and into the channel. The day was unusually clear and the water sun-kissed as they departed the sand dunes; the coarse beach grass stirred in a welcome breeze. Maryetta took one last look at the church-spired horizon and the great sea walls fading from sight, and wondered at the repetitious scenes of her young life. Familiar things, loved things ripped away—the plains of Iowa, the brick house in New York, and now the land of the Belgae.

She remained at the railing, oblivious to the other passengers, until someone spoke.

"Pardon me, but have we not met?"

Maryetta turned to face Nigel Edmunds, the man who had been her teacher on the Oostende sands! The gray hair was now pure white, but the complexion was the same—clear and as youthful as she remembered. And the voice—that too was the same.

"Monsieur Edmunds! How wonderful to see you again!"

"It has to be three—maybe four years?" he asked. "You have grown up, Maryetta Cobbet!"

"Yes, sir. I have finished school."

"And how does it happen that you are going to Dover?"

He spoke kindly, just as she remembered—as a father might.

"I am returning to my own country. I am going to America."

The news seemed to please him.

"I have prayed for you, Maryetta, more than once."

"But I do not go to my father's home. He is too busy for me."

Nigel Edmunds frowned and shook his head.

Maryetta went on. "But you, are you leaving your ministry in Oostende?"

"No. My work has grown in Oostende. I now have a new field—in Brighton. My spinster sister lives there and helps with the work."

Maryetta smiled, remembering their first conversation and how he had avowed that the world was his parish.

"And is the work in Brighton growing?"

"Yes, though it is small but, I assure you, promising. I get assistance often from my colleagues who attend the Pastors' College.

Have you ever heard of Charles Spurgeon?"

"No, monsieur, who is he?"

"A most remarkable man. Makes it possible for men like myself to study the Bible. But even more—his lectures! His comprehension of the Scriptures is most inspiring."

A long silence, and then he seemed to realize that a young girl might not be too interested in Bible college lectures and exposition.

"It must have been difficult to leave your friends at the convent."

"Yes. I shall miss them."

"Especially your sister—what was her name?"

"My dear Sister Celeste died, monsieur in the dreadful epidemic. I recall you thought God had sent her to me." She paused. "Why do you think He took her away?"

The look on the young girl's face warned Nigel Edmunds that he had better proceed with Holy Spirit wisdom and godly compassion.

"That is difficult to answer, Maryetta—very hard. We humans live so close to our sorrows. But I do believe that when we see the entire picture clearly it will be different. St. Paul said that 'we see through a glass darkly' but then—'face to face.' We must lean on the promises of God, the assurances that beyond this vale of tears lies an open gate—a gate only for those who have made Him Lord of their lives. I think, too, that if we could even catch a tiny glimpse of the world beyond, we would not cling so hard to those who are called away. There is no sorrow there—no pain—only peace, joy, and comfort for eternity. I am sure your Sister Celeste is in a new place, blessed of God—and waiting for you and understanding the mystery of it all."

"I am sure too, monsieur, that if ever a soul were to be canonized a saint, it should be my dear Sister Celeste."

The preacher looked beyond Maryetta when he replied.

"Not all saints are canonized, child. I have known many, many uncanonized saints—some Catholic, some Protestant, and some neither. God's records read differently from ours. He alone knows His sheep—and they know Him."

"You seem to have no bias."

Water had splashed onto the railing from the sheerline, where the vessel had cut the waves. The preacher put a finger in the salty drops and stuck it in his mouth.

"Taste it," he said, "and tell me—is it Catholic salt or Protestant salt?"

Maryetta smiled slowly. "You do not hate Catholics?"

"Hatred has no place in the heart of a true believer. We do not see denominational lines, we see people as lost or saved. We love as does our Lord."

"Then why the divisions? I hate divisions."

"I do not look at divisions as something always evil. I see the godly warriors of each age keeping the faith pure. God does raise them up—He has always raised up contenders for the faith as it is laid down in His Word. Apostles of truth as taught by our Lord Jesus."

"But what is truth?"

"Hmmm—the question of the ages! It was asked by a Roman governor once. Men, honest men, have earnestly sought to know it—and have found it too. The American Emerson seemed to think the search for truth was a disease. Your great president Lincoln counted on it to vindicate slander. I think that truth is a tiger that ungodly men refuse to face, but I let the Scriptures answer the question. Jesus said in His great priestly prayer that God's Word is truth. It is the touchstone whereby all philosophy is measured. Truth breaks the shackles from the brain and body and sets a man free. Jesus said it would. I have experienced it, as have countless millions. Ah, but I see I confound you, and I apologize. Someday I trust you will understand more. Right now I must walk. Will you join me?"

Maryetta declined and watched the man walk away. She did not see him again until the great white cliffs of Dover came into view, when he appeared and offered to carry her valise.

"Will you go on from Dover?" he asked.

"I must. My ship leaves Southampton in five days."

"Then again we say good-bye. May I wish you Godspeed, Maryetta, as you travel, and blessing in your new life."

LATER, STANDING ON THE dock wondering where she might inquire for a coach to Brighton, she felt loneliness creeping in again like the fog that was shrouding the seaport. She felt that alien isolation that one feels in a crowd and wished that Nigel Edmunds had not left. There was about the man a peace and a confidence that had a spirited contagion—it was the same magnetism Sister Celeste had possessed.

She found the inn where lodging awaited her. Early the next day, she climbed aboard a coach and reached into her purse for the sandwich she had purchased.

Two women and an elderly gentleman were already within, and in a short time the driver climbed atop, rocking the vehicle violently under his excessive weight. The wheels began to turn, and the coach was off. They had not gone far when they came to an abrupt halt.

"One more passenger!" shouted the driver, again rocking the coach as he swung down to open the door.

Nigel Edmunds entered the cab, and with him a welcome ray of sunshine.

"Sorry," he said, "I could not go on to London without doing what I was sent here to do."

The other passengers took him to be an eccentric bloke and gave him cold stares. Where he chose to travel was of no consequence to them! But Maryetta knew he was speaking directly to her.

It was past noon when they approached the seacoast towns. It was Rye first, with her protective gates and cobblestoned roads. They passed droves of sheep and Norman stone churches and were then on to Hastings. Nigel Edmunds narrated to Maryetta the history of each particular site until she could almost hear the clash of Saxon and Norman sword. The passengers chafed, but that did not discourage Nigel Edmunds. He was keenly aware of the young girl's fears, traveling alone and contemplating the distance she was to travel. He would supply diversion as best he could.

When they entered the environs of Brighton, a brisk wind came up. The early novelty of traveling had long since lost its charm. Maryetta grew tired and found she could take little interest in viewing the regency houses they were passing.

Arriving at an inn, both she and Nigel Edmunds got down from the coach and stood observing as their unfriendly and dignified traveling companions greeted relatives. Maryetta could see that Nigel was searching the serried crowd.

A very attractive middle-aged woman made her way toward them. She, too, had silvery hair and a flawless complexion.

"My sister Margaret," explained Mr. Edmunds, graciously introducing them.

"Have you made arrangements for lodging, Miss Cobbet?" he asked.

"No, but I shall find a place."

Instantly the sister seemed to sense Maryetta's confusion.

"May I offer my home, Miss Cobbet? It will be much better than an unfamiliar tavern—and you do look worn."

Maryetta opened her mouth to decline and looked into the darkness of the city with hesitancy.

Nigel Edmunds took advantage of her hesitation. "Yes, please do come. You still have a distance to travel."

"You make it difficult to refuse."

"Then it is settled!" Margaret Edmunds linked arms with Maryetta and led her to a waiting carriage.

The Edmunds' home proved a delightful place, not far from a rocky beach and reflecting the warmth and hospitality of its owners. Maryetta enjoyed a late supper and was taken to a pleasant room overlooking the water. It was another night away from the convent, away from the little narrow bed she had so disdained at first. Now, she would have given most anything to be crawling into it. She fell asleep with tears drying on her cheeks and with a determination to leave the next day with a braver spirit.

When morning came, Maryetta arose in the silence and semi-darkness of dawn. There was a feeling of tropical air as she dressed and ventured outside. She walked along the coarse pebbled shore enjoying the respite from constant travel, the opportunity to exercise and to view the beauty of the place. As she retraced her steps, she recognized her benefactor coming toward her on the beach.

"Ah—I see an early riser!" was his greeting.

"Oh, sir, you have a heavenly place here. I do so appreciate your kindness."

The preacher raised a hand of protest.

"We are honored to have you as our guest. We thank God for the opportunity to send you on your way refreshed and with a prayer."

"Someday I shall learn to pray, but you know, I do poorly with prayers. And now I have no intercessors."

"You have the greatest Intercessor who ever walked the earth! Did you never hear the words Paul wrote to Timothy?"

"I do not own a Bible. What did he write?"

"By divine guidance he wrote, 'There is one God and one mediator between God and man, the man Christ Jesus.' "

"I don't feel worthy of that."

"Nor should anyone. That is where the grace of God enters in."

"My! You *are* a preacher. Did Jesus Himself say anything about being that presumptuous?"

"Indeed He did! He said, 'Whatsoever ye shall ask in my name, that will I do, that the Father may be glorified in the Son.' "

"What does 'in my name' mean?"

"It means by His authority. We don't go into God's presence

because of who we are, but because of who Jesus is and what He has done for us. It is always His name that opens the gates of prayer."

"Protestants seem to have great freedom. I can appreciate that."

"Another promise He has kept: 'If the Son therefore shall make you free, ye shall be free indeed.' "

Nigel Edmunds was looking at the well-worn Bible in his hands. Impulsively he held it out to Maryetta.

"Take it, Maryetta. I am convinced our meeting was no accident. It does seem that our Lord is drawing you to Himself. If so, you must read this. Right now I would like to pray for you."

Maryetta was impressed with the man's sincerity and his intensity. He was already closing his eyes.

"Our Father, grant this child a true knowledge of Yourself. Remove every hindrance, every devilish stumbling block and set her feet upon the sure foundation—Your Holy Son. Cleanse away her sin and her bitterness as she yields to You, and by Your mercy see her safely to America and ultimately—someday—to her home with You. Amen."

Maryetta was surprised by the brevity of his petition and touched by his gentle solicitude for her well-being.

"And now, come—you shall have a good breakfast to start the day's travel."

AS THE COACH PULLED away, Maryetta looked at the Bible and then back at the good man and his sister. It was evident that God thus far had blessed her with journeying mercies. Such watchfulness did encourage one to trust Him for the days ahead. This man's God seemed to be a caring God, the God she wanted to know.

But the preacher had said that hatred had no part in the heart of a believer, and Maryetta was not ready to relinquish that. She would face Lydia now that she was able. She would make her confess to her lie. This time Lydia would not be facing an innocent child, but an equal!

The countryside was vastly different from the level topography of Belgium. Maryetta's brief stay in London at eight years of age had done little to impress upon her young mind the lush verdancy of England—the grassy meadows, the quiet ponds, the meandering rivers.

From her cramped position in the coach, she could see fields of buttercups and clover and envy the wandering sheep for their wide berth of grazing land.

The black and white half-timbered inn facades were well designated with coats-of-arms, either genuine insignias or chosen for their heralded fables. Always there was someone in the coach to recite the history, to spin yarns of residing ghosts, cats—red-coated soldiers, kings, wenches, and lepers—who still haunted the post-stations.

For three nights Maryetta was obliged to put up in such places, where she spent her hours awaiting a visit from the ugly phantoms. Then, up early and back on the road by dawn, she was glad to be free of not only the roving specters but of the ribaldry coming from the central rooms where the men drank their weaver's ale and rudely discouraged sleep.

From Brighton the coach rolled and rambled on to Worthing and eventually arrived at Southampton. There was little time to view the port, but somewhere Maryetta had heard that this was the place from which the Pilgrims had departed England.

Relief flooded Maryetta's being as she walked up the gang-plank and settled into her small quarters. She could now freely anticipate the wonders of the New World—leave the Old with only a flimsy suitcase and a French accent, enjoy the ocean voyage, rest and relax, and be thankful she had come this far with no problems.

What would it be like—meeting her grandfather and Ellen, and again seeing American shores? America—what would America be like now?

12

THE GREAT SHIP SAILED OUT OF THE CHANNEL AND INTO THE broad Atlantic, embracing the golden days of July. Even the nights were wondrous as the vessel plowed the silvery, moon-splashed waters.

In these rare leisure hours Maryetta read from the Bible Nigel Edmunds had given her. Her friend had said that God was drawing her, and there was no question that as she read there was a stirring of interest in a world greater than the one seen with human eyes.

She often thought of her Grandfather Downing, feeling an impassioned gratitude toward the man who had, without ever laying eyes on her, opened his heart and home. What would their meeting be like? And the meeting with Ellen at the New York station?

At long last the modest skyline of New York came into view.

This is a very young city, thought Maryetta. None of the gray pillared columns and stone heights of Gothic structure, no heraldry and no monarchical system. Worlds away from Belgium.

Dozens of European emigrants stood at the railing, viewing the land upon which they had set their hopes. The ship docked and they poured down over the gangplank, gawking in wonder and running into the arms of waiting relatives. Maryetta wound her way through the cacophony of strange dialects and on to a waiting depot wagon.

As they neared the Central New York station, her heart began to beat wildly. Would she even recognize her old friend? Entering the bustle of thronging travelers, Maryetta scanned the faces. Then she saw her!

Standing alone and looking abashed at the pedestrian traffic was her beloved nurse. She was wearing an enormous hat, doubtless one from a former age, retrieved from the depths of an old trunk. She was searching the myriad of faces as they crowded past her, hoping to see something familiar—blonde curls, possibly, or square-lidded gray eyes in a round face. Knowing that her nurse could never imagine the changes maturity had made, Maryetta slipped in behind her and placed gloved hands over the older woman's eyes.

"My sweet darlin!' " exclaimed the little Scot, rolling her "r's. Turning, Ellen looked into Maryetta's eyes. "I'd know me Maryetta anawhere!" she declared.

All Maryetta could do was cry and move into the warm, loving arms and listen to the familiar brogue as Ellen sputtered out her thanks to God for the reunion.

Still holding to Maryetta's hand, the old nurse walked Maryetta to a cafe, all the while unable to take her eyes from the beautiful young woman beside her.

"The Cobbet gray eyes!" she exclaimed. "They've never changed!"

Maryetta refrained from asking the question that time had never answered, but only until they had settled themselves at a table.

"My father, Ellen. Do you see ever him?"

"Aye, lass, we sometimes meet. He lets me know when his travels takes him near me town."

"He still travels?"

"Aye, though he doesna stay long in ana one place. Always the traveler, back and forth he goes—New York, California, sometimes Washington, D.C."

"Do you know where he is now? I should like to see him while I am here."

"The papers say he is off for Europe. I clipped it out. Here, let me see. . . ." Into the oversized black purse she plunged her chubby hands.

"Ah, here 'tis. Mercy—he left yesterday!"

Maryetta knew instinctively that the timing had to be Lydia's. The scheming woman had scored another victory. Now it would be months before she could confront her parents, and she would be at the end of her money.

"Oh, Ellen, has she never changed?"

"No, lass. But here's another clippin' I thought t'would int'rest you. She's allus managed to be in the high-society column, but lately the news folk seems to be a-pokin' fun at her—the way she treats her servants. Says here, she embarrasses 'em—sending 'em to get crop gleanings! And her a millionaire!"

"I thought her servants were treated well."

"Yer stepma doesna treat anabody well for long, love. Y'should know that!"

The conversation continued, and Maryetta told about her years at the convent. Then, seeing a train conductor turn down a station board, she arose, promising to return to New York and make definite plans to meet with Ellen again.

"Y'don't have y'father's New York address, do y'now?" Ellen rummaged in the black purse again. Finding the penciled address, she placed it in Maryetta's hands and embraced her.

As Maryetta disappeared with her small suitcase into the mouth of one of the big gray cars of an east-bound train, she glanced back and saw a small figure sadly watching and waving.

CHANGING TRAINS IN BOSTON, she settled into the hard yellow seat as the train roared on toward her destination. It was the last leg of her long journey, and Maryetta was not only weary, but heavy of heart. When would she ever see her father?

The unfamiliar odor of bituminous coal flooded the car from the open doors. The train seemed to be flying past so much that she wanted to see—steel bridges, graveled roads, the heart of fields and forests, small farms and weeping willows hanging over reflecting ponds! Gone were the canals, the vineyards, the cathedrals and castles, and in their place were strange little white churches, rolling hills, and unfamiliar vegetation. It was hard to realize that she had been in this new country before . . . but what a good feeling to know that it was her country—young America!

The conversation around her arrested her attention—the clipped English—the Yankee twang—the absence of "r's—the creation of extra syllables where one should be. Maryetta wondered if her grandfather spoke in this strange manner.

The country's economy had apparently recovered from the Civil War debt, for the folk sitting close by seemed very well dressed. Shyly she let her gaze encompass the nearest travelers—and found herself looking into the luminous, dark eyes of a young man seated opposite her.

Something decidedly foreign to Maryetta stirred within her, and she crimsoned. The man looked every bit a gentleman and seemed as surprised and flustered as she. Even though the glance had been swift, she had made observations.

He was some taller than herself, though not a great deal, and was dressed extremely well. His eyes were intelligent, penetratingly beautiful, and he had thick dark hair, a well-structured face—strong chin and nose—and a well-trimmed mustache. When she looked his way again, he seemed engrossed in his newspaper.

The ride grew long, but the expectancy of meeting her unknown relative kept Maryetta nervously alert. She could not relax, and she was earnestly hoping she could act the part of a lady when the meeting took place. She must quiet the inward trembling, appear unshaken. Life did seem to be a wearisome camouflaging of true emotions!

She had grown accustomed to the conductor bellowing out the names of the stations, but when he announced "New-bree-poht," her nerves became unraveled and she could not stop shaking. She arose much too quickly and struggled to retrieve her valise from the overhead rack. Barely able to reach it, she gave a gasp of frustration.

"Let me help!" the gentleman across the aisle quickly offered.

His face was much too close to her own, and she blushed again and murmured a thank-you.

"You have traveled a long way," he observed, looking at the tags on the valise.

"Oui, monsieur, I have come from Belgium."

"You are French—er—Walloon?"

"No, sir. I am American."

"But your accent?"

"I have been away for a very long time. Now I come to live with my grandfather."

"Here in Newburyport?"

"He lives in Byfield. He has directed me to get off here."

"What is his name? Perhaps I know him."

"His name is Nathan Downing. I am Maryetta Cobbet." And she curtsied.

"Well—welcome to America, Miss Cobbet. I am Matthew Haddon. Perhaps I can help you find your grandfather. The name is familiar."

The train was already passing between giant-sized steel doors and triggering the ear-splitting bells. The clanging noise was deafening.

Soon Maryetta was down on the platform looking dazedly at the steam writhing around the big wheels—and puzzling at the strange design of the town's station. She had never seen a small, rural train station where a train might pass through colossal gates and right into the station itself.

Already the driving rods were moving the train on.

She looked about wildly for the face she had never seen, hoping her grandfather was one of the group come to meet the train's passengers.

Suddenly Matthew Haddon reappeared at her side.

"Don't worry, Miss Cobbet. He is probably on his way. If he does not come, I will see that you have a way to Byfield."

A fair-haired young girl came running toward them, and beside her a blond youth. The two were apparently brother and sister, for their features and coloring were much alike. Impulsively, the girl embraced Matthew Haddon, exclaiming repeatedly how wonderful he looked. It was plain she had not seen him for a long time.

"Come, Matthew, the wagon is out back. Oh, you do look so professional!"

Matthew appeared to be embarrassed, but he courteously introduced the young people to Maryetta.

"My little sister, Miss Cobbet, and my brother, Joshua. Bethia, this is Miss Cobbet. She has come from Belgium."

"Belgium! How exciting! Are you visiting?"

Matthew answered for her. "No, she has come to live with her grandfather in Byfield."

In the distance, Maryetta could see a berry-colored wagon approaching in a cloud of dust. A white-haired man sat on the seat, bent upon moving his pair of bays. He was heavy set, built like the Dutch farmers of Limburg. He pulled the steeds to a halt and got down from the wagon, searching the platform.

As he approached their little group, he stared at Maryetta, his eyes as wide open as his mouth.

"You are my June all over again!"

Dutifully shaking her hand, he lifted her suitcase onto the wagon.

"Come! 'Taint much of a chariot—but gets us there."

Realizing that her travels were over, Maryetta was able to smile. She wondered if she would ever learn to speak the dialect of her grandfather.

Following his directive, she climbed aboard the buckboard where she sat stiff and terrified. Holding to her hat with one hand and to the seat with the other, she departed the station in much the same fashion as her grandfather had arrived.

MATTHEW HADDON WATCHED THEM go, clearly disappointed that he had missed an opportunity to learn exactly where Maryetta Cobbet lived.

His sister observed him with fascinated curiosity.

"We met on the train," he explained quickly before she could ask. "But let's get on. I am anxious to see Father. He does keep well?"

But his eyes remained on the vanishing buckboard, and his astute sister could see that he was far more interested in the young lady from Belgium than in the health of their father.

"I thought you didn't like girls!" said Bethia with her usual lack of diplomacy.

"Who said I do now?" was the retort.

Bethia's amused expression, had Matthew troubled to take note, would have told him that he did not deceive her!

13

ONCE ON THE TURNPIKE, THE HORSES SETTLED DOWN TO A reasonable pace and Maryetta was able to relax her grip on the rough wooden seat. The scenery now absorbed her interest; so much wilderness, so many miles of marshland with haystacks dotting the land like great golden beehives.

When they arrived at the wooded swales, the sweet fragrance of pine lay heavy in the air and the warm sun seduced the cleaving laburnum. She wondered at the graceful white birches and the wild tiger lilies—wondered too, if Americans picnicked as often as did the Europeans. Did they skate on the ponds in winter as the Dutch did on their canals? Surely they must, for the land was so full of lovely watered places.

They traveled for what seemed an eternity with no human life visible. They had not even passed a house for miles. Then they turned in to what appeared to be primeval forest, and the road became more of a narrow wagon path where cathedral pines touched branches with overhead oak and elder to form delightful arches. Unfamiliar vine and brush scraped the sides of the wagon.

A few houses came into view. They were small, though well crafted, and almost all of them had built-on sheds and ells.

Grandfather tipped his hat to several folk as they rode along, so Maryetta felt certain they were nearing his home.

"Center of town's up the road a piece from where we live. 'Taint much of a place, Maryetta," he said by way of apology for the primitive surroundings. "I'll take y'there after you're settled."

Abruptly, as seemed to be his way, Grandfather Downing turned his horses in at a steep incline, and the house that was to be Maryetta's new home came into view.

It was a nice house, stretching over a broad parcel of high cleared land. Grandfather had said that he was a cabinetmaker. It was also evident that he knew something about carpentering houses!

A short, stout lady emerged from a side door and hastened to greet Maryetta. Her floor-length flowered apron was besmudged with flour, and she tripped repeatedly in her haste.

"Welcome, dearie!" she called.

This was Grandma Trudy, her grandfather's second wife. Her real name was Gertrude, but as Grandfather had referred to her as Trudy, so would Maryetta.

Inside, Maryetta stared at the rough-hewn open beams that gave the place an impression of spaciousness. The kitchen seemed large with cabinets to spare. A soap stone sink boasted a large black pump, and she could see herself grotesquely reflected in the nickel of the kitchen stove. Everything had been polished to a welcoming brilliance. Clearly, her grandparents had outdone themselves in an effort to please her. Something cooking on the stove reminded Maryetta that she had not eaten for a long time.

Grandma Trudy noticed her lingering glance at the steaming pots and spoke. "You must be hungry, child, and mighty worn down. Soon's you see to your room, we'll have a good meal."

Grandfather Downing carried her valise to a closed door and set it down. He fumbled in his pocket for a key and clumsily unlocked the door. Entering the dark room from a sunny kitchen made it difficult for Maryetta to see the interior.

"This was June's room. Hasn't been changed since—well, we don't move furniture much. Seems fitting you should have it."

He walked around the furniture as though he were seeing it for the first time. It gave Maryetta the impression that the place had sacred memories—memories her grandfather would prefer not to disturb.

"She kept it mighty purty—sewed, crocheted things—samplers, tidies."

Maryetta could only assume that the room had been closed off since her mother had left home. She began to appreciate the fact that here was someone else who had shared in the grief of losing June Downing. A swift rush of stinging tears made her turn away from her grandparents and face the windows.

"May I?" she asked, reaching for the curtain pull.

"It's your room, Maryetta."

At the invitation, she pulled on the cord. The drapes swept back, revealing a scene of such natural beauty that she gasped. The windows themselves were expertly crafted, framing the outdoor scene. Multi-paned with deep sills, they looked out upon a prolifically blooming garden.

"Oh, Grandfather, how utterly charming! May I keep the drapes open?"

"As you like."

Maryetta walked around the room, touching things she had not seen at first. She stopped to admire the huge fireplace and looked at a photograph on the white pine bureau.

"This is Mama, isn't it?"

Grandfather Downing nodded his head in answer, then walked to the door.

"Come now. Trudy's got the table set."

Maryetta followed him to the big kitchen where dishes lay steaming on the table. From their ample number, it was clear there must be a garden nearby.

They sat down and waited for Grandfather to return thanks, then ate in an appreciative silence.

Helping Trudy clear away the dishes after the meal, Maryetta spoke.

"You are a wonderful cook, Grandma Trudy. I hope you will

teach me some of your Yankee secrets."

Grandma Trudy smiled. "That will come, dear. Right now I'd like to see you resting. A good night's sleep should do you wonders."

Maryetta did not refuse the suggestion. Returning to her room, she began to dust the furniture with her pocket handkerchief. Suddenly she was overwhelmed by the awareness that this was a part of her mother's life, one she had never known. She stretched out on the bed and buried her face in the embroidered sham.

Oh, Mother! If only you had lived, how different my life should have been! I could have known my grandfather and visited this lovely place often!

Quietly she thanked God for her safe arrival, her new home, and the love being shown her, then speedily she drifted off into an exhausted sleep.

WHEN MARYETTA AWOKE, the sun was streaming in at the pleasant windows and a red-breasted robin was swelling his throat with a morning song. She lay watching him as he added a dance to his tune. The strident sound of the cicada, too, lent its voice to the morning matins and with sibylline accuracy forecast extreme heat for the day.

Maryetta was appalled to discover that she was still in her clothes and that someone had covered her with a sheet. Rising, she found also that water had been placed in the dresser pitcher and clean towels beside the huge round bowl.

Attired in fresh clothes, she made her way to the kitchen, where she found a note on the table directing her to a pot of cornmeal on the stove. The Yankee "maizena" was much to her liking. She ate in silence, washed the dishes, and stepped outside.

A dry, dusty odor hung in the air. Summer suns were doing their ancient old work of drying and ripening, just as in Belgium. Chickens were foraging for slugs and thistle-seed, softly clucking their appreciation and contentment. By a Virginia fence the morning glories bloomed profusely. She could see both grandparents at work in the fields.

They have so little, she mused, yet they are willing to share what they have with me. Why could not my stepmother have been as gracious?

AT NOON GRANDMA TRUDY came to the kitchen, her arms overflowing with vegetables. Placing the colorful assortment of tomatoes, beans, corn, and green things on the drain board, she began to clean them with a small brush. Maryetta joined her, washing the vegetables under the pump and trimming them.

Trudy moved quickly through the routine, formed from many years of practice. She packed her jars, placed them neatly in a basket, and headed for the door.

"Where are you going, Grandma Trudy?" asked Maryetta.

"Too hot to can in here. Got water already on the cookin' stove out in the summer kitchen. Come see."

Grandma Trudy walked ahead out over a field and into a lath-work enclosure. There on a strange looking homemade stove stood an enormous copper kettle. Trudy placed her jars inside, wryly commenting that the Almighty had once again blessed the vines of their high-ground fields.

"And now, Maryetta, I think you should spend time with your grandpa. I want you two to get to know one another. You'll find him in the big shed over yonder." She pointed in the direction of a large building.

Grateful for Trudy's sensitivity, Maryetta thanked her and crossed the wide field to the designated place.

Upon entering, Maryetta could see that her grandfather was deeply engrossed in some sort of woodcraft. The smell of new wood filled the room with a delightful sweetness.

At first she saw only the cabinet he was working on, leaning heavily on it with what appeared to be a plane. Then she realized that in the deeper shadows of the shed were superbly crafted pieces in various stages of completion. One beautifully crafted escritoire looked out of place in the old building.

"Oh, Grandfather! You are indeed a cabinet maker!" She ran her hands over the satin finish.

Grandfather Downing looked up from his labors and studied his granddaughter. It had been a long time since any such youthful person had entered his workshop or admired his work.

"Y'like it?" he asked.

"Oh, yes, and this one too! They are beautiful—beautiful!"

"Y'can come along with me when I deliver them Monday."

Maryetta was sure that none of the simple homes they had passed in Byfield would be housing such magnificent furniture.

"Where do you sell them?" she asked.

"New-bree-poht," he answered absently, going back to his work.

"You go there often?"

"Ayuh. My customers live there."

Maryetta walked about the building, examining the tools and admiring the handiwork. She took notice, too, of her grandfather's rough, gnarled hands and threadbare clothes.

"I—feel I must speak to you, Grandfather, about something important."

"Ayuh?"

"I wish you to know that I intend to carry my own weight. I shall look for employment at the first opportunity."

"Didn't 'spect that when I asked y'here. Y'can help Trudy—that'll be 'nuff. 'Sides—y'aint bigger'n a peanut. Even a mild Nor'easter'd carry y'off."

Maryetta grinned but was not discouraged. "Is there a local newspaper?"

"In New-bree-poht. The Haddon fella who came in on the same train as you used to be the editor, 'till he went to Washington, D.C. Been there a number of years. I think he's back for his old job. Most folk don't leave this place—leastwise not for long. Something 'bout it draws like a magnet once it gets in yer veins."

"You know his family?"

"Ayuh—real old family. Father runs a dairy—good respected folk."

Maryetta turned away from her grandfather's curious gaze, harnessing her desire to ask more. She could still see the luminous dark eyes and the way Matthew Haddon had looked at her—could still remember how she felt when he had reached for her valise.

"And stores? Are there dry-good stores in Newburyport?"

"Ayuh—they's several. Trudy'll take y'there come Monday."

Back in her room, Maryetta counted what remained of her money. After her traveling expenses there had been very little left, and she had never been more in need of clothing. Now there would not be the luxury of the bolts of brown material with which to make a new uniform, nor the white English cotton with which to make underclothing.

Going to Newburyport was an event she could readily appreciate. She could advertise as well as purchase yardage, and perhaps she could settle into her new surroundings with a measure of confidence.

WHEN THE DAY FOR the promised trek arrived, a neighbor came to join his strength with that of Maryetta's grandfather in loading the heavy cabinets onto the old buckboard. They blanketed and tied them securely and were early off to the old "Port city."

Maryetta was far less apprehensive of the driver and the lively horses than she had been the first day. This time she could be more attentive to the New England landscape. Quail and partridge scampered before the grinding wheels, and squirrels scolded from treetops. The wood thrush and the redstart blended their songs in early morning matins, and ducks flocked down upon the crystal ponds, making small talk with one another.

On the turnpike they passed leggy pine swales, oak, beech, and scrub willows. Seagulls flew in from the ocean, decrying already the heat of the day. Wagons turned out in increased numbers as they drew near the old city.

Grandfather Downing turned his horses into a street called High and reined them in at one of the great three-storied federal houses. The fan lights, porticos, and Palladian windows were all new to Maryetta. The architecture was in a way linked to the Yankee's ancestral Old England, only with small differences—doubtless because of limited funds, or possibly because the early settlers desired individualism and a certain freedom from monarchical directives.

The August sun had failed to rob the green from the sweeping terraced lawns; they stretched all shadowy and verdant before the great houses. Surely, the Yankee had set in wooden edifices a rare and quaint design that would mark the city for centuries. Given time, one might forget the ancient wonders of Europe and grow to like the fine doors and blooming gardens.

Male servants came to carry the heavy desks and cabinets indoors while Maryetta and Grandma Trudy waited in the wagon. Grandpa Downing emerged from each delivery with an expression of extreme satisfaction and a quick salting away of his well-earned greenbacks. The money would see them through the hard winter months to come.

When they headed for Market Square and the business section of the city, Maryetta noticed that the traffic picked up considerably. Each traveler was intent upon enjoying a profitable bit of old Yankee bartering.

She observed that even with a pocket full of money, Grandfather Downing was extremely prudent about spending it. She must do something and quickly if she were not to be a burden. Asking directions and gaining permission, she was soon heading up a steep incline to where the city's business offices were located.

"We shan't be leaving for at least another two hours," called Trudy after her.

Maryetta needed no more encouragement. She walked up the street, peering in at the windows, dallying before ship chandleries, surveyor's offices, attorney's offices, bookstores, and an apothecary shop, until she reached the place she had hoped to find. The building was painted yellow, and on the front glass door she made out the letters "The Morning Bugle."

As she opened the door, her presence was heralded by ringing bells. She looked up and saw the bells dangling on a spiraled spring. A young man came from the rear of the building, smelling strongly of printer's ink. He ushered her into a well-kept office.

"I wish to advertise in your paper," said Maryetta.

Laboriously he copied out her words on a thick pad of paper and told her the price.

With a heavy sigh she paid it, then left the newspaper office in search of yardage stores.

MATTHEW HADDON CAME INTO the news office later and looked over the stack of advertising slips.

"Where did you get this?" he asked the young man in the rubber apron, holding up a slip of paper.

"A young lady brought it in."

"When?" he demanded.

The fellow shrugged. "I don't know. Close to an hour ago."

Matthew looked at Maryetta's well-formed signature and read the ad: "French lessons (private or class) weekday evenings and Saturdays by appointment. Inquiries answered by mail. Address to Maryetta Cobbet in care of Nathan Downing, Byfield, Mass."

Matthew rewrote the ad and placed the original in his pocket, where it remained for several days. The feeling of it there stirred a restless interest.

When Saturday arrived, he harnessed Dandy and headed for the turnpike. He was sure that someone in the neighboring town would know where Nathan Downing—and his pretty granddaughter—lived.

14

Bethia Haddon watched as her brother drove the wagon down the long driveway and out onto the road. He'd been hitching the wagon at precisely the same hour each Saturday now for nearly a month. He had also changed his usual Prince Albert style of dress to a more flamboyant fashion.

"I think our brother is in love," she confided to her older sister, who was visiting.

Caroline looked pleased. "I cannot think of anything better for him. A good wife could make quite a difference in his life."

By September the beautiful rare Indian summer days had arrived—days that made the heart sing. The skies were clear and the air brisk—not a cloud to be seen. Asters were beginning to appear by the roadside, and hornets were buzzing about busily seeking a winter hideaway. Men were in the fields and orchards harvesting the last of the crops, pitching hay and talking about the coming river regatta. It was an event few citizens of the Port city would miss if they could help it, and the Haddons were no exception.

A change in Matthew's mood, however, seemed to be putting the damper on Bethia's enthusiasm for the community event.

"Things going along well at the paper?" asked Bethia, concern marking her expression.

He nodded his head noncommittally.

"Then what's got your feelings by the tail?"

Matthew ignored her question. "What sort of gift does a young lady like?" he ventured.

"You have a girl?"

"Bethia, you do ask questions!"

"Well, I should like very much to see you interested in a girl. Who is she?"

"I do not 'have a girl.' I simply want to show my appreciation to a very fine teacher."

"What teacher is that?"

"A French teacher."

"Aha! The pretty Miss Cobbet! I thought you had noticed her!"

Matthew shrugged his shoulders. "Unfortunately, so did a number of others. Her classes are overflowing, and I daresay studying a foreign language is not the primary interest of many of her students."

Bethia placed her hands on her hips and looked at her brother in exasperation.

"Well, you saw her first! Come now, Matthew, faint heart ne'er won fair lady. You have as good a chance as anyone. Buy her flowers—perfume—anything, so she'll know you are interested."

"You think that could make a difference?"

"Oh, men! How can they be so dense?! How is a girl to know that a man has noticed her unless he gives some indication?"

"I had not thought about it that way."

Bethia wasn't finished. "Who are the others?" she asked.

"Tom Hale, Arthur Rummel, Isaac Timens—to name a few."

Bethia whistled.

"What's that for?" asked Matthew.

"They could buy her the town!"

He turned his back toward her. "I know."

It was clear that Matthew did not welcome his sister's entry into his hopeless situation. But Bethia understood her brother better than he knew, and where Matthew was concerned was willing to rush in where angels feared to tread.

"Matthew, don't give up without a fight. Ask her somewhere—ask her to go with you on the *River Queen* the day of the regatta. I hear there are still tickets."

"She'd never go!"

Bethia was losing patience. "Then don't ask her. Just sit and watch while someone with more gumption steals her right out from under your stupid nose!"

THE DAY OF THE regatta arrived—yet another delightfully crisp, early autumn day. The town folk flocked to the river banks. Boat enthusiasts and shipbuilders would have their day! The ladies were decked out in their sporting best, the small boys wore sailor suits. Folks came in droves, a sea of bright colors, carrying blankets and picnic baskets and sloshing jugs of lemonade.

The Haddons were there, too, all but Matthew, who had unobtrusively excused himself from the enthusiastic throng. Bethia stood at the water's edge with her cousin Allen and a man named Drake, a person her father had saved from certain death during the War between the States.

A mackerel breeze tossed shreds of white clouds over an azure sky and drove little black divots into the river's crested surface. Ocean gulls soared above, attracted by the noise, the color, and the sure possibility of picnic remnants. The boatswains were already beginning their parade down the swiftly flowing Merrimack.

Crafts were peopled with crew, guests, and family, the occupants as flagrant about displaying their summer finery as the captains, who displayed their colorful flags.

Among them came the two-masted barques, the square-rigged Thomas vessels, whalers with oil-stained sails, smoky steamers, and dozens of small craft. Some ships had come from as far away as New Hampshire's Tilton and Franklin. Horns sounded and bells rang; skippers on board doffed their hats, to the delight of small children on shore. Soon brightly colored tablecloths were spread along the banks, and the picnic baskets were opened.

Joshua walked to the edge of the lapping waves with his father, but Bethia kept herself busy setting out a tempting assortment of food. When a murmur went through the crowd, she looked up to see a large craft coming into view.

It was the *River Queen*, well bedecked with colorful standards. Women in white skirts and colorful scarves and men in straw hats and bright blazers crowded the rail and waved.

Bethia glanced anxiously over the decks, then saw what she was looking for.

"It's Matthew!" she exclaimed with delight.

"Matthew—on the steamer?" replied Allen. "Why, look! Who on earth is the beauty next to him?"

"The little Belgian girl, that's who! Oh, Allen, isn't that grand?"

Indeed! There stood the shy, unassuming Matthew Haddon—and beside him Maryetta Cobbet, obviously enjoying every moment!

15

OCTOBER CAME ON WITH THE FIRST NEW ENGLAND FROSTS, followed by the creeping fogs of early dawn and evening. The deciduous trees began to display their riotous colors, and Maryetta viewed the spectacle with awesome wonder. She had no recollection of ever seeing such colors, either in Europe or in Iowa.

Grandfather began to speak of the severity of the winter that lay ahead, explaining that the coming months would halt all passage on the roads. The snow would bring to an end the popular French classes, but that was nearly a month away.

The success of her classes was a source of pride for Maryetta, as well as a means of paying her board. If the weather were to be as severe as her grandfather predicted, she would have to revert to something else. She would buy good material and fashion some clothes in the latest European styles. Before winter, she would make it a point to model them as she applied for part-time work with a seamstress.

The idea had struck her on one of her first trips to Byfield's small center. It was just as Grandfather had said—"down the road a piece and not much of a town." Dwarfed and limited in number of buildings, its merchandise running a poor second to that of the industrious Port city, it probably would never grow beyond its tiny post office, general store, small white church, little red schoolhouse, grain store, and blacksmith's shed.

At the town's edge, in the front window of a private home, she had seen a large sign announcing that the occupant was a dressmaker. It was not likely that she would be hired, for Grandma Trudy said that the woman was a war widow, entirely dependent upon her skill as a seamstress. She would not likely have anything left over from living expenses to pay for hired help. Still, the possibility was there, so Maryetta summoned her courage and went to pay a call on Mrs. Stuart.

The dressmaker opened the door and smiled pleasantly, but when she learned the object of Maryetta's call, her attitude changed abruptly.

"There is hardly enough business to care for one," she explained.

But Maryetta would not be daunted. "But if there were two sewing, there should be double the income—and you, being the proprietor, would be entitled to three-fourths of the increase." With her eyes downcast she continued, "I had so hoped my training in Europe might be of use. We were taught much in the art of design and style."

"You were trained in Europe?"

"Yes, I was sent to a Belgian convent for my education."

Mrs. Stuart looked at the fine lines of the suit Maryetta was wearing.

"You made this yourself?" she asked.

"Yes."

"Well . . . I'll tell you what. We will try two days a week come November and see what comes of it."

MARYETTA WAS ELATED. Now she could continue paying her board and relieve her conscience of ever being a burden to her grandfather! Of course, the hours with her new family would be curtailed. She was reveling in the feeling of belonging and loved it when her grandfather introduced her as "our granddaughter" or "June's little girl."

There was a certain aloofness about the neighboring Yankees;

they kept their affections for long-standing friends and relatives. But hope stirred in Maryetta's breast that someday she would make lifelong friendships with folk her own age—perhaps with the Haddon family members. Theirs seemed such a close-knit fellowship, the kind she had always longed for.

And the elder brother, with his gentlemanly European good manners and endearing shy ways—she thought about him a great deal. He had come to her classes humbly and quietly, only for her to discover that he had already mastered Latin and Greek. She thought about his lack of self-worth. A woman could change all that, could make him believe in himself. The equivocal trait sent danger signals to her heart and she made definite plans to give him more personal attention.

There was also Tom Hale, the overconfident romantic, a handsome fellow with a dreadful pride! She had accepted his invitations at first, until he had begun to assume that she was his girl exclusively. When she repulsed his aggressive overtures, he had become surly.

Maryetta secretly wished that Matthew had some of Tom's confidence—but she could not dwell long upon the situation. Already the demands of her new work were growing. It had not taken long for word to spread that Mrs. Stuart had a European stylist working for her, and the two days a week increased to four and eventually to the entire week.

Before her move to Grandfather Downing's, Maryetta had seldom had the luxury of evening reading. Now she missed it. She thought often of Nigel Edmunds and his encouragement to seek after the scriptural promises . . . but now there was no time.

With the end of October came the dying and the drying of green things. Leaves fell from the trees, were raked and heaped into dusty heaps and set on fire. They sent an acrid odor wafting into the sharp fall air. Pumpkins and apples were harvested, and winter clothes came out of attic trunks. Trudy hung hers on the line to dissipate the strong naphthalene odor.

Maryetta could not help but view with dismay the sad display that hung in the open air. Hardship had no courtship with pride, and it was clear that for her grandparents, clothing had run second place to more necessary items. Indeed, everything the little woman wore looked as though it should have been sent to the rag bag long ago. At Maryetta's first opportunity she would rectify that.

Still—with all of little Grandmother Trudy's penury, she had a glow on her face as she went about her day's work. Years of "making do" had not robbed her of a happy countenance or rosy cheeks.

With the starlings in the yard in increasing numbers and home preserving well underway, Maryetta began to see why the old Franklin stove was such a cherished piece of furniture. For while it boiled jars and sent spicy aromas through the entire house, it also provided a delightful warmth that was deeply appreciated in the cold of the mornings and evenings. Sitting down to Trudy's nourishing meals and later watching Grandfather start up the fires in the wide-mouthed Rumford fireplaces were the most welcome moments of her day.

The first snow fell in November. It was not too heavy a snow, and the oxen-drawn sledges had early "broken out" the roads. Grandfather, who had prepared and painted his cutter, spoke of taking his granddaughter for her first New England sleigh ride. They would make a special trip to the city on her one afternoon off to buy winter staples and view the holiday displays in the store windows. He wanted to look over the latest in farming equipment, and Trudy was interested in the crockery stores. This gave Maryetta some welcome time to browse alone—not to purchase anything, but just to see the latest.

She dressed warmly, wearing two sweaters under the old winter coat she had brought from Belgium and the "make-do" pair of galoshes Grandma Trudy had retrieved from a box in the attic. Maryetta hoped that the small red rose she had basted on the underside of her ruche bonnet lining might keep folks from noticing her old galoshes.

She had not seen Matthew since the closing of her classes. Would he think her bold if she stopped in at the newspaper office? After all, they had been together on the *River Queen*. The desire to see him struggled with her inbred propriety for a very brief time, then she headed up the steep incline to the newspaper office.

Matthew had seen her coming and was holding the door open. She stepped inside, stamping the snow from her borrowed galoshes.

"Maryetta—what a surprise!"

She was satisfied that she had not made a mistake in coming. Matthew was friendlier than she had ever seen him.

"I've wondered about you. How are you getting along since your classes have come to an end?"

"I have found other employment. Every day except Saturday afternoon and Sunday, I work with a dressmaker."

"Then you will stay here in New England?"

"Of course. Did you think I would not?"

"I had hoped you would stay."

They talked of weather and world events and very little that interested either of them, until Matthew took a deep breath and inquired, "Do you have special plans for Christmas?"

"Oh, it is more than a month away, and well it may be. Our clients are loading us down."

"It isn't too far away to make plans. Would you and your grandparents consider having dinner with me—with my family? They will all be there—"

Maryetta's gray eyes sparkled. "How kind of you! I would love to come, but of course it will have to be my grandparents' decision. If they were to receive a written invitation and were agreeable—perhaps I might send you a note?"

Matthew's expression said more than his words. "We have our Christmas dinner at two o'clock, but please—come early."

Maryetta left the office with a lively step, already mentally sewing a Christmas dress and thinking of ornaments to put in her hair. She would make up something nice for Trudy, too!

16

THE GRANDPARENTS TOOK WELL TO THE IDEA OF SPENDING Christmas afternoon with the Haddon family. The long hours at the dressmaker's home should have left Maryetta no energy to do her own sewing, but the thought of spending the holiday with Matthew was enough to fire her energies, and the long hours seemed as nothing!

Christmas day dawned upon the little community with the profusion of ringing church bells. At first Maryetta thought she was awakening to the bells of Brussels, then she realized where she was. This was Christmas day in America!

The dressmaking had been concluded as well as the making of small gifts for each of the Haddon family members. Maryetta stood looking at the photographs on her bureau and wondered about former Christmases in her grandfather's home. What had the bells meant to her mother? Had there been a Christmas tree in the parlor—stockings hanging at the fireplace—plans for a Christmas dinner?

And the meaning of Christmas—was it really just the giving and receiving of gifts, family reunions? And what about reunions? Was her beloved Sister Celeste experiencing reunions in heaven? Would the day come when Maryetta could embrace her beloved friend? Had not the One whose birthday was being celebrated made such reunions possible?

The paltry gifts of earth seem as nothing compared with the promise of eternal life that that first Christmas had meant to a world lost in its damning sin. Yet how was it possible that heaven's ruler could be sent in the form of a tiny baby—restricted to a human body—and been so willing to give His life for man's reconciliation to God? Peace to men of goodwill—God's will—peace that would lift the hopes of men to something high and holy. Already Maryetta had felt the tug of His sovereignty.

As Maryetta dressed she could not help but let her thoughts wander back to the convent and to her second Christmas there, when Sister Celeste had changed a nightmare into a blessing. She could see her blowing up the coals, ordering her to cut the Greek bread, feel her agile fingers making curls in her hair.

Where are you, my beloved friend? Are you with my mother? Do you see the face of Jesus? Do you know what goes on here?

Her thoughts were interrupted by Trudy's call to breakfast. Grandfather had gone to work early with a lantern and later had appeared in his Sunday best, looking sheepishly to the women for their approval. Or perhaps it was the shy delight he was feeling as he presented his granddaughter with a huge, brightly decorated box. Both he and Trudy stood with shining eyes as they watched Maryetta open the box and withdraw from its depths a heavy beaver coat, a warm fur bonnet and muff to match, new gloves, and new galoshes!

Maryetta looked from the gifts to the delighted givers with her mouth open and tears ready to spill over. She knew that such extravagance had robbed these dear people of many necessities and that she must keep her emotions from taking control or they would think her ungrateful.

Sensing her struggle, Trudy spoke. "There now, girl—try them on. I was careful to get the right size, but let's make sure."

A little after noon, Maryetta slipped into her scarlet dress. Trudy unearthed an inexpensive ornament for Maryetta's hair, and Maryetta presented her grandmother with the lovely serge suit she had spent so many hours on. Together, they stood admiring one another's holiday attire.

"I have packed my best fruitcake!" exclaimed the little woman, her voice shrill with expectancy and her cheeks rosy with excitement.

Cold, brisk winds had made their unsolicited entrance upon the happy season, whipping energy into the restless bays and coloring nose and cheek with color enough to rival the basket of apples packed in the cutter. Maryetta and her grandparents drove off to the delightful sound of sleigh bells and church bells, gliding smoothly over the white forest path and on to the turnpike. Holiday excitement was evident everywhere as they passed dozens of sleighs and waved to their occupants. The store windows in Newburyport still boasted of unsold treasures, displaying bright ornaments, candy canes, sleds, drums, dolls, and sugarplums.

The sleigh came to a halt at the great front door of the Haddon home. It was hung with a huge wreath, and the night's frost had iced it and made the red ribbon appear even brighter. Matthew was standing watch at the front door and came quickly down the front steps, calling out holiday greetings over the din of the barking dogs.

Grandfather's expression showed mild approval as he watched the young Haddon fellow welcome his granddaughter, and he sent an unguarded wink in Trudy's direction. Tall young Joshua took the horses, and the little party entered the house.

Maryetta felt instantly the hospitality both of the charming old house and the fair-haired Bethia who came to take their coats. In the parlor stood a giant pine tree, its top scraping the ceiling and its branches strung with cranberries and heavy with bright old ornaments. With a pang of nostalgia Maryetta thought of the festivities of the old New York brick house, but she shook the memory away.

They were politely presented to the master of the house, Clinton Haddon. Maryetta, studying his kindly face for a long time, could see that he was the strength of the family. At once he put Grandfather Downing at ease with farm talk and an invitation to visit his barn and see his growing herd of cattle. Grandma Trudy gravitated to the big Haddon kitchen, where she proudly presented her own baked offering and joined in the busy work going on there.

Matthew left Maryetta only long enough to replenish the fires, then returned quickly to explain the treasures of the Haddon family that made their appearance only at the Christmas season. Holidays past seemed linked closely with the holiday present.

"My sister will be here any minute. I am anxious for you two to meet," he said.

"You have a sister besides Bethia? I didn't know."

"Yes. Her name is Caroline."

"—and your mother?"

"Mother died at the end of the war."

Maryetta sobered. "I was five years old when my mother died," she stated.

Matthew could see that he had clouded her thoughts and moved to undo the damage. "Come! You haven't met Aunt Phoebe and cousin Allen."

He led the way to the kitchen where Trudy and Aunt Phoebe were bustling about in animated fervor, appreciative words tumbling from their lips as they fussed over steaming pots and sizzling pans.

"Aunt Phoebe, stop for a minute. I want you to meet Maryetta."

Phoebe gave the young girl a fleeting glance, wiped her hands on her apron, and mumbled a curt "Howdy." She seemed none too pleased with Matthew's timing.

"May I help?" asked Maryetta.

"Good gracious, no! Any more folk in this kitchen and we'll be standing on each other's shoulders! Matthew, see what you can do to clear the place—" Her eyes suddenly fastened on Joshua. "And you, Joshua, get your hands out of the plum pudding!"

Joshua made a wry face at the fuming woman and left. He was clearly not too fond of his bossy aunt. The young people hastened back to the parlor to continue their visit.

Cousin Allen was a warm sort of person, not at all like his rude mother, and endeavored to make Maryetta feel welcome by asking earnest questions about her years in Brussels. His younger sister, Clara, didn't speak much but clung continually to Allen's side.

Bethia was the friendliest of all. She walked Maryetta through the rooms of the house and made her feel the most important of guests. They stopped before the old parlor organ.

"I must see how dinner is coming along, Maryetta. If you know how to play this thing, please do—something Christmasy and jolly!"

Maryetta had not expected such a privilege. The sight of the old square organ with its yellowed keys stirred memories of her brief musical study in Brussels.

"I haven't touched the keys for months. Do you really want me to?" she asked.

"Yes, yes. Go on."

Gingerly Maryetta sat down on the crewel cushion top and began to pull out the stops. Soon strains of music were filling the house and drawing its occupants to the source. Maryetta's heart and hand took wing—Gauntlet's "Once in Royal David's City," Handel's "While Shepherd's Watched Their Sheep by Night"—the music delighting them all.

Bethia came from the kitchen with eyes aglow. "Oh, Maryetta, don't stop. It's beautiful!"

Encouraged, Maryetta went on and became so engrossed that she did not hear a carriage entering the driveway. She picked up on the tempo and began to play and sing some of the little French tunes Sister Celeste had taught her.

Suddenly she was not singing alone. A man's voice had joined with hers. Assuming it was Matthew, she thought mischievously to challenge him. She would sing an old whimsical French song—and she would sing it in its original language!

Surprised that her partner kept singing right along with her, she finished with a flourish and a giggle.

"Somebody knows French!" she exclaimed, whirling about on the stool. But instead of seeing Matthew, she found herself looking into the strong face of Jerome Cavell. Each stared in unbelief.

"The Conservatoire!" exclaimed Jerome with unabashed delight.

Color rushed to Maryetta's face, and she covered her mouth with a shaking hand.

"Monsieur Cavell!"

"Go on, mademoiselle," encouraged the genial artist.

"Oh—I could not!" Maryetta got to her feet.

Maryetta stood stunned, staring first at the unexpected guest and then at the Haddon family members, who by now had gathered with as many questions as were on Maryetta's tongue.

"Maryetta from the Brussels convent—and so grown up!" continued the great gentleman. "What a surprise—and what are you doing here?"

"I—I—"

"She has come to live with her grandfather," explained Matthew, duty-bound to champion Maryetta's cause. "He is here, too. Come, we must make introductions,"

The color had deepened on Maryetta's face as she realized that she would have to explain why she had not gone to her father's home.

But remembering their past conversation, Jerome quickly relieved her of an explanation.

"I see your father did not send for you," he said quietly. "Do not speak of it now. This is a great occasion. Come, you must meet my family!" Graciously he led Maryetta to a corner of the room where a beautiful dark-haired woman was standing.

"Caroline, meet my little Maryetta. She is the child who gave me the rose. Maryetta, this is my wife. We have prayed for you many a night in our evening prayers."

When the lovely woman spoke, Maryetta thought her voice extraordinarily gentle, stirring memories of her own mother.

"How like our wonderful Lord to bring us together, and in such an unexpected way! Welcome to the Haddon household!"

A young child who might have been four years old came and pressed her face into the folds of Caroline's dress.

"I would know at once that she was yours," said Maryetta, studying the delicate features.

"Yes, except for the eyes. They are Cavell—much to her father's delight and approval!"

"It is that way with me, too."

"Tell us, Maryetta, how is it that you have come to Newburyport."

Bethia interrupted the conversation by announcing that dinner was ready, and they all gathered around the big table. Maryetta was overwhelmed with the generous spread. New Englanders seemed to lack nothing when it came to food.

She was impressed, too, with the way the presiding host was reverenced, for each gave him undivided attention as he opened his big yellowed Bible and read of the Savior's lowly birth. After reading, he bowed his head and prayed, his strong, commanding voice directed straight to his God. Like Nigel Edmunds, he seemed to be on intimate terms with the Father.

"Lord of heaven, be our guest at this our family table, and grant us that same blessed grace when the day ends and the shadows fall. May there never be one of us absent from Your holy supper.

"Now, please bless this food and the hands that prepared it and receive our gratitude for your constant and faithful provision."

Cousin Allen came with a huge, golden bird on a very large platter and set it ceremoniously before Clinton. Laughter and conversation mingled with the carving and the feasting. Allen and Jerome seemed engrossed in talk of farming techniques, and Maryetta inquired of Caroline why a concert performer should be so interested in farming.

"Jerome is taking a year off from his travels. He wants to enjoy a little family life, which it seems he never had much of as a child. We have bought a small farm in my grandmother's old town, Boscowen. We will work it through the spring and summer."

"I should think that quite a transition for your husband," said Maryetta.

"Yes, but I am sure he will adjust. Difficulties disappear when one wants to learn."

Matthew sat quietly observing and appreciating the manner in which his family had welcomed the Downings.

At the head of the table, Clinton was tapping a silver spoon on a cut-glass sugar bowl. On his face was a sly, amused expression.

"Hear ye, hear ye! I do believe Aunt Phoebe has an announcement!"

Phoebe blushed, though not shyly. It was obviously a moment she relished.

"We have set no definite date," she said with practiced modesty.

"Tell us, Aunt Phoebe!" prodded Bethia.

"Well, ah—we shall be married some time in the spring—Mr. Paine and I! We've been seeing one another ever since he bid on my box lunch at the church social!"

She paused, waiting for the family's reaction. When the others registered their delight, she proceeded.

With an air of triumph, she said, "Of course, we are not in a hurry to make this public—not until we've been seen together a few times. We shall live in his mansion—on High Street."

"Is it important to live on High Street?" asked Maryetta quietly, turning to the youthful Joshua at her elbow.

"It is to Aunt Phoebe!" answered Joshua, a trace of contempt in his voice.

"Hush, Joshua. Don't spoil her little moment!" whispered Bethia.

Allen, Phoebe's quiet son, spoke to his mother. "We are all pleased and happy for you, Mother."

Phoebe looked satisfied, and Allen went back to his silence. Somehow, he seemed apart from the gaiety—thoughtful in a sad sort of way. Bethia, ever sensitive to the feelings of others, thought it a good time to throw another bone into the family's midst to chew on.

"Uh—has anyone noticed that Matthew has acquired a little more education?" she asked.

"How is that?" asked Jerome.

"Tell them, Matthew."

As usual Matthew looked impatient with Bethia and thoroughly embarrassed.

"He is speaking French quite well now," explained Bethia.

"Not really that well, Bethia. But what progress I have made has been due to the patience and the efforts of a very capable teacher."

The compliment went straight to Maryetta's heart.

"Matthew is much too modest. He learns quickly—a student any teacher would appreciate."

Once again, Maryetta felt the dark eyes upon her, saying things she wanted to hear. She wondered what it would take to loosen his tongue.

"Has the transition been difficult for you, Maryetta?" asked Jerome. "The language, the change of countries, and all?"

"There have been times when it was difficult, and I have had to struggle to remember my English, but I am learning again."

The conversation went on around her, and Maryetta pondered the silence of the withdrawn Allen. After leaving the table, she questioned Matthew about his cousin's disengagement from the family's conversation.

"It is a long story. Allen has a brother, Timothy—a twin—and there has been a quarrel."

"Where is the other brother?"

"Went to New York months ago. He thinks Allen stole his girl, but we don't believe it. Allen is a man of character and wouldn't do anything so shoddy. We think it was Lindy who broke up the relationship with Timothy."

Maryetta was disappointed to find a flaw in the family she so looked up to.

Matthew went on. "We would like to see a marriage for Allen, but there is something there I don't understand. I think he is in love with Lindy but won't admit it. He'd never hurt his brother deliberately."

"Do you think a marriage would help him?"

"Yes, a good marriage has a way of building a man—completing him."

"Your sister Caroline—she seems to have that complete marriage."

"Yes. She does have a good marriage, now. Though she and Jerome each had to realize that the other was an individual. Her experience has taught us all a great deal."

After dinner, Allen invited Matthew's guest to visit his stable.

They crossed snow-encrusted fields where the footing was treacherous. Maryetta went along, slipping and sliding and hoping she would not be a spectacle, but Matthew seemed to enjoy her dependence upon him. They remained at the stable for a long time, enjoying the conversation and camaraderie until it was time to leave.

Matthew took the opportunity to press for another meeting in January.

"New Year's Day, perhaps?" he asked.

"Yes, but you must come to Byfield."

The wonderful afternoon came to an end with a fresh flurry of snow and a chorus of good-byes. The Downings drove off into the chill of December's cold with warm thoughts in their hearts.

17

WITH THE ARRIVAL OF JANUARY, THERE CAME MANY CHANGES. Snows settled in, blanketing the entire countryside but not keeping Matthew Haddon from getting the cutter out and driving Dandy up the turnpike to Byfield. He spent many days with Maryetta, sleighing, exploring, and explaining the idiosyncrasies of the New England winters.

"I may not see you again until late March." he said as he prepared to take his leave one afternoon.

Maryetta waited for an explanation.

"February is our worst month. It grows colder—and the blizzards! The roads will be impassable, and we are inclined to hug the fires."

"You cannot mean that it gets even colder than now!" Many a night already Maryetta had dragged the throw rugs from the floor of her room and placed them on her bed for extra warmth.

"I'm afraid so," he replied.

Maryetta looked appalled. Never in all of her years at the Belgium convent had she been subjected to such frigid weather.

THE FOLLOWING DAY Maryetta bundled up in her warm clothing and went as usual to take up her sewing at Mrs. Stuart's. The woman was waiting for her at the door and did not welcome her inside.

"I am sorry, Miss Cobbet, but I shall have to let you go. With the holidays over, there won't be enough work to keep even one of us busy."

Chagrin and anger mingled their venom and displayed themselves on Maryetta's features. She well knew that Mrs. Stuart's clientele had more than doubled since she had come to work for the woman.

Her employer quickly added, "Come back in March. We shall have Easter sewing to do."

So saying, she retreated, leaving Maryetta staring blankly at a closed door. Her disappointment was matched only by her outrage. The woman was not only unfair and unfeeling, but rude as well! Now how was she ever to pay for her board?

Grandma Trudy met her at the farmhouse door with her usual comfort, a comfort Maryetta was beginning to lean upon more and more with the passing of time.

"I am surprised," said Trudy with Down East-simplicity. "Don't she know 'bout the law of res-tee-tu-shun?"

Maryetta had never heard of that law, either, and looked questioningly at her grandmother.

"It's an unwritten law, Maryetta. Sow good seed—good will grow. Sow bad seed, and reap a crop of failure. Mrs. Stuart will some day reap the worst from her actions!"

"How can that be, Grandma Trudy? I brought her so many new patrons. I don't see how she could possibly lose out."

"You'll see, honey. God is not mocked. Y'don't mess around with God's laws, lest y'want t'come up on the short end."

"But it seems to me that I'm the one on the short end."

"Y'haven't seen the end yet. Sometimes what looks like defeat turns t'something better."

When Grandpa Downing heard of the dismissal, he surprised Maryetta by displaying delight.

"But I won't be able to pay my way," complained Maryetta.

"As I already told you, y'not to concern y'self with such things. You are here because we want you. Now we'll have a spell of time to really get acquainted!"

"Well, when spring comes, I'll have my language class again . . . and someday, I'll have my own business!"

GRANDFATHER WAS RIGHT; the long winter months brought the three an opportunity to get better acquainted. February blizzards came as predicted, bringing with them blessings and satisfactions Maryetta had seldom experienced.

She watched spellbound as neighboring farmers hitched their oxen to brightly painted wooden sledges and went about breaking out the roads. It was not unusual to see four pair of the beasts pulling one sledge, though often all that Maryetta could see beyond the high drifts were the massive heads and wreaths of steam pouring from their nostrils. Once a large ox-drawn "chebobbin" full of logs came into view, with nearly a dozen noisy young schoolboys standing aboard as weights.

Snowshoes came out of the barn along with the cutter, and Maryetta was introduced to a geniality and pleasure she could not have imagined. Sleighing and woodland treks became the order of the day, and when the heavy snows cut them off from all living, there was a comfortable settling in beside roaring fires with a goodly number of books, including Whittier's "Snowbound" and Walt Whitman's "Leaves of Grass." Grandma Trudy seemed always to unearth the unexpected from secret storage places. The season took on an interest and new meaning to Maryetta and stirred afresh a feeling of being part of her own country.

Little things—fox tracks and fence shadows on virgin snow, a trickle of brook water showing through heavy mounded snows, overburdened pine limbs nearly touching the ground, blue jays scolding—stirred the artist's soul inside the young girl. The scenes awoke her love for painting, and she opened her old valise and brought out her watercolors and oils. Both grandparents stood by, expressing their appreciation for Maryetta's talent.

The opportunity to spend time painting proved Trudy's prophetic observation that Maryetta had not seen the end of events. She recalled something that Nigel Edmunds had read her from the book of Jeremiah. Vaguely it came back: "For I know the thoughts that I think toward you, saith the Lord, thoughts of peace, and not of evil, to give you an expected end."

Always, there seemed to be a voice—a soundless voice—calling to Maryetta, and she pondered the words over and over. The "expected end"—what could it be?

The hiatus of the winter months gave Maryetta time to think and wonder . . . to think about Matthew Haddon and to wonder what was going on at the Haddon farm. Meanwhile, she exchanged letters with Bethia and waited for springtime.

BETHIA AND MATTHEW, whose natures were diametrically opposite, had never been close, so it was with more than a little satisfaction that Bethia began to appreciate her sibling's interest in the letters Maryetta wrote her. An avowed romantic, she was not only in favor of the match but was a willing advocate for Cupid. When Matthew would ask casually what was going on in Byfield, she would dole out just enough information to tease.

"Maryetta really has a sense of humor, Matthew. She insists that if it gets any colder, she is going to cave up with a hibernating bear. She thinks being eaten alive could be no worse than freezing to death."

Of course the pragmatic Matthew saw no humor in the situation.

"I was afraid she would have difficulty adjusting. I wish there was something I could do to help. She should not have to suffer so."

Mischief spread slowly over Bethia's fair features. "Maybe you could marry her!"

Bethia had expected Matthew either to explode or ignore her. Instead he stood looking at her, and she knew he was weighing his thoughts and his response before he countered. She braced for the duel.

"Is marriage always the solution for you women?" he asked.

"Well, it does seem to be a universally accepted practice—and a practice from which most red-blooded men do not shy away!"

"Be careful, little sister, not to confuse discretion with cowardice. If a man does not take into account his ability to manage a household, he could be letting a lot of innocents in for some very bad times!"

"You sound like Papa!" exclaimed Bethia, impatient with her practical brother. But his reaction had told her what she wanted to know. He had been thinking of marriage!

Matthew was smiling, pleased that he had riled his emotional sister. Besides that, he thoroughly enjoyed a debate! And he had an opportunity to teach her a small lesson in good old Yankee conservatism!

But he hadn't needed Bethia to put the idea of marriage into his head. From the first day he had set eyes on the Belgian charmer, Matthew had thought of little else. By the end of March, he was walking the wet and windy streets of the little city of Newburyport, checking out houses advertised on the market. Almost all of his Washington, D.C. earnings he had put into savings, so with his secure position with the newspaper he felt able to entertain thoughts of marriage—unless, of course, the lovely Maryetta was not interested!

His search took him repeatedly past a quaint gambrel-roofed dwelling on a street called Fairlane. Its antiquity had sparked his interest, and its proximity to Newburyport's business section also had an appeal.

The branches of two full-grown chestnut trees reached long arms over the roof, not unlike his own Haddon homestead, sheltering it from winter snows and summer suns. He could almost see leafy shadows playing over the white cedar shingles come summer.

Former owners had planted laurel, linden, and mulberry trees behind and along the side yard, with fruit trees in the back. A grapevine had been trained over a high whitewashed trellis. Morrow honeysuckle, too, climbed over side door trellises, and he recognized lilac and Catawba rhododendrons along an old stone wall.

He decided to place a bid on the property and sent a note to Maryetta expressing a desire to see her on the first warm Saturday.

"I THINK IT WOULD be best, Maryetta, if you settled on a definite date and invited your Mr. Haddon to an early dinner," suggested Trudy.

"Wouldn't it be too much expense—and work?" asked Maryetta, unable to conceal her enthusiasm.

"It would be neither, dear, especially since you would be doing the cooking and the serving!" There was mischief in Trudy's smile.

"You would let me do that?"

"Of course!"

Maryetta turned the bright prospect over in her mind, her expression taking on a rare glow.

"Why, Grandma Trudy, I could make up my own personal menus as I learned to do in the convent . . . cook a true continental dinner—*Witloof—Anguilles au vert—*"

"What in the world are *witloof* and—that other Angwee-stuff?" asked Trudy.

"You Americans have a funny way to say it. I think you say 'cheekaree.' And *Anguilles au vert are eels.*"

Trudy shivered. "Not on my table, if you don't mind!"

But Maryetta wasn't listening. To plan what she knew best how to cook and serve—and to have Matthew Haddon as her dinner guest—was more than she had imagined possible.

April days came on with fluctuating temperatures. Close to May, the first signs of spring began to appear. Pale green buds were swelling on the stalks of daffodils, and bird songs were flooding the early dawn. Maryetta's heart was singing a new song too, as she went ahead with her dinner plans.

"See, Grandma Trudy, I have finished the menus. There will be one for each of us."

Trudy looked at the embossed folded cards and exclaimed over the fragile little violets Maryetta had painted on them.

"I've put the date in the corner, see? May 6, 1871. I think I shall want to remember this date."

Trudy looked puzzled. "Why do you make lines between the foods?" she asked.

"Because, Grandma, they are courses."

Grandpa Downing came and looked over Trudy's shoulder. "Courses?" he asked, making a wry face.

"Yes, Grandpa, we are served seven times."

"Great Caesar's ghost, Maryetta! We'll never eat that much!"

"Oh, you do not understand. We do not serve great heaping dishes, but small portions. We make dining an adventure!"

"It will be an adventure, all right!"

MATTHEW HADDON DROVE THE horse up the steep incline, and Grandpa Downing went to greet him. While Grandpa took the horse to shelter, Trudy opened the door. Maryetta joined her, dressed in flattering blue with a frilly white apron.

Both women raised their eyebrows when they caught sight of Matthew's new suit. He had broken away from the drab colorless winter clothing and was sporting a bright blazer and a much too early straw. He came toward Maryetta smiling and handed her a bouquet of roses.

He watched for her reaction and was not disappointed, for she gushed and thanked him enthusiastically—but could he see more? Could he see an interest in himself?

"Maryetta has done all the cooking, Mr. Haddon. Says it's European. And since it is all strange to me, I think it best if we just excuse her and let her play hostess her way."

Maryetta left them in the parlor and went to work with her finishing touches.

The dinner proved to be exceptionally good. Even Grandpa Downing had to attest to that, though he murmured aside to Trudy that he was still hungry.

After dinner Trudy, beaming with pride, placed her napkin on the table and addressed Matthew.

"I think it would be nice if Maryetta showed you around. Grandpa and I can clean up."

Maryetta sent her a look of gratitude and went for her coat.

"We can walk to the pond now—it isn't frozen over anymore!" she said to her guest.

"Bethia tells me you are not adjusting very well to our winters."

"Your winters are frightful, Matthew. I do not know how I shall survive another! They are a real challenge to me."

"But where could one go to escape?"

"I am seriously thinking that I must make an effort to visit my father. He would know how to advise me, especially since he has lived here longer than I."

They were entering a fringe of forest, both taking note of the flora and fauna, enjoying the growing things they hadn't seen for months.

"I have wondered, Maryetta, why you did not go to him in the first place."

Inbred loyalty struggled against Maryetta's need for flesh and blood empathy. She opened her mouth to explain and found she could not.

"You need not tell me if you don't want to. I didn't mean to pry."

Maryetta looked into the warm brown eyes and thought how easy it would be to confide in this man. Still, the years of disappointment had built a protective wall, and for some reason she was not ready to trust anyone.

"I'm afraid the only ones who really want me are Grandpa Downing and Trudy," she said with a laugh, trying to make light of the situation.

But Matthew had stopped walking. He turned to her and took her face in his hands.

"You must know that isn't so," he said soberly.

And before she could answer he was kissing her.

Even with Janine's explanation of "love's first kiss," Maryetta could not have dreamed of its dimensions. When Matthew released her, she stood looking at him, blushing and speechless.

But Matthew wasn't speechless. Everything he had ever wanted to say to Maryetta came tumbling from his lips.

"I have wanted you ever since that first day at the train station. I was never more disappointed in my life than when your grandfather showed up!"

"What are you saying?" The gray eyes were wide with wonder.

"I am saying that I love you—I want to marry you."

Maryetta looked puzzled. Hadn't Janine spoken of diamonds—music—candlelight? Was this the way Americans proposed a marriage?

"Why are you looking at me like that?" asked Matthew. "Why don't you say something?"

"You are making a proposal?"

"Of course I am making a proposal. Have I done it wrong?"

When Maryetta still remained silent, Matthew began to entertain qualms.

"Tell me," he demanded.

"I—I—thought when a marriage proposal was made—there were things like—music—and candlelight—"

She was looking at Matthew, her eyes as direct and honest as a small child's.

Matthew sighed with relief.

"Oh, is that all! Truthfully, I had not planned it to be at all like this. If it's music and candlelight you want, I promise you, you shall have them all."

Satisfied, Maryetta laughed and lifted her face to his and in her kiss, gave him his answer.

On the rest of their walk, they saw nothing but one another—savoring the sweetness of first love with arms entwined.

"I have been looking at houses," confided Matthew. "When you are my wife, you will never again be cold. There will be wood aplenty and fires going in every room!"

"Let's go back and tell Grandpa and Grandma," suggested Maryetta.

"No, let's wait until I get an answer on my offer for the house. Then we shall have more to tell."

"I don't think I can keep such a secret."

"It won't be for long."

"As you wish," said Maryetta, savoring the feeling of belonging at last, of having a real partner. Loved by someone who wanted her for life—the homing pigeon—the last piece of a puzzle!

18

BY THE END OF MAY, BETHIA HAD GUESSED THAT SOMETHING momentous had taken place in her brother's life. The cool-headed, factual Matthew was noticing things he had never noticed before. He was even practicing his good manners on her! He asked questions about women, too—something quite out of character for a man who hitherto had seemed to have all the answers.

"You aren't telling me something, Matthew," she commented one morning.

"How right you are!" he rejoined. "And I do not intend to, little Miss Inquisitive!"

"Well, all I can say is—whatever is going on, it is quite obvious it agrees with you. It's making a human being out of you."

Matthew looked at her, his expression softening.

"What are your plans for Sunday?" he asked.

"Nothing definite. Maybe a walk to Newton's Pond—cream toast for supper."

"Well, you can plan a walk with me—into town."

Bethia brightened. "You are going to be nice?"

Matthew grinned. "I am nice!"

Bethia waited for Sunday the way a child waits for Christmas. She was sure that now she would get to the bottom of Matthew's change of behavior.

The early amaryllis were already in bloom and catkins were thick on the big-toothed aspen leaves when the two walked into town.

"Don't you just love the spring?" exclaimed Bethia, holding close to her brother's arm.

It was clear that Matthew's thoughts were not on the beauties of spring. He didn't answer until they had turned into Federal Street, walked to Spring, and then headed down Fairlane.

"Come," said he, stopping at a low white wooden gate.

He walked down the path and produced a key from his pocket.

"Is this yours?" asked Bethia, wide-eyed.

"Not yet, but it will be!" Matthew said in a nonchalant way.

"And you have kept it a secret!"

"Well, you know the old sayings about counting chickens and slips twixt the cup and the lip."

They entered the parlor, a large sunny room that ran the depth of the old house.

"It smells like paint," commented Bethia, enjoying the clean odor.

"I insisted on that."

Bethia's mouth had widened as well as her eyes. "Matthew Haddon! You are going to get married!"

"Yes."

"Oh, Matthew, how utterly wonderful. When?"

"We haven't set a date. I took a risk, put in a down payment with the stipulation it would be forfeited if I changed my mind—which of course, I would never do."

"Has Maryetta seen the house?"

"No, but she knows about it."

Bethia shook her head.

"Honestly, Matthew! Don't you know you should have shown her first?"

"No! I wanted suggestions from you."

"That's the nicest thing you have ever said to me. What is it you want to know?" Bethia savored her brother's rare approval.

"It's colors. You know I am not much at such matters."

"Just keep to neutrals. Maryetta is very artistic. She'll know what colors to use. But I do wish you had brought her here before. I think she will be disappointed that I have seen her house first, and I wouldn't have it that way—not for one minute. I think of her as my dear friend."

"Come, Beth—what is the difference?"

"Really, Matthew, you know so little about a woman—" said Bethia impatiently, "the things that hurt and the little things that please."

It was difficult for Bethia to reconcile her abhorrence of Matthew's hard-headed nature with her genuine love for him. There had always been that inexplicable something lacking in him—something she was certain would in time catch up with him . . . and could bring him to his knees. She did not want that. She changed the subject quickly.

"When will you know the house is yours?" she asked.

"Possibly in a month—perhaps a little longer."

He looked thoughtfully from a row of windows. "Maryetta will want a garden. She loves flowers."

THE WEEKS THAT FOLLOWED were weeks unequaled for brother and sister. The shared secret developed into a sweet fellowship and a light heartedness they both enjoyed—an occasional wink, a quiet exchange of words.

Then one day Matthew came home from the office with a look on his face that Bethia had not seen since he was a young teenager—the same look he had worn when he brought news years ago of the War between the States beginning.

Their father, as he often did, had invited his close friend Drake Singleton to dinner. He seemed to need the close fellowship of his former war buddy, and Bethia usually looked forward to the man's cheerful fellowship. But tonight she wished Drake were not there; she wanted to question her brother, and could not do so if it exposed him to any embarrassment.

She prepared the supper and kept up the conversation, hoping to allay any suspicion that Matthew was troubled. He remained outside the conversation, but this was not entirely out of keeping with his nature, and the others thought nothing of it. He excused himself early and sought solitude in his own room. Whatever was bothering him, it was clear he preferred not to discuss it.

The family retired early as usual, but Bethia found it impossible to sleep. She slipped into her bathrobe and went to the kitchen for a glass of milk.

When she went through the sitting room, she sensed a presence there. A closer look revealed Matthew sitting in the Boston rocker; the moonlight coming in at the window illuminated a picture of a dejected man.

"Matthew, you aren't in bed."

"Obviously."

"What is wrong?" asked Bethia.

"Everything!"

"You didn't get the house?"

"It is much worse than that."

Matthew hesitated, but his sister pressed on.

"Please tell me. You know I will help if I can."

"It's the newspaper."

Not understanding, Bethia waited silently.

"It has been sold. The new owner will be the editor—they do not need me." He gave a great sigh. "I should have stayed in Washington. I would have, if I had had any inkling that this could happen."

"You don't mean that, Matthew."

He was silent.

"How will that affect your buying the house?"

"I've had to withdraw—can't make payments without income. I have forfeited the down payment, too."

"Does Maryetta know?"

"No. And I shall not tell her."

"But you know she would wait."

"Would she? She is already thinking about going to her father in New York. That would be better than waiting for me. I don't have the right to keep her waiting."

"Tell her, Matthew. Let her make that decision."

"—and let her know what a complete idiot I am?"

There it was again—the wavering . . . the lack of confidence . . . and the pride!

"Then tell her you have made a decision. Don't leave her in the dark, dangling and not knowing what it is she must deal with."

Matthew rose and came close enough that Bethia could see his expression, which was anything but brotherly.

"You stay out of it, Bethia—you hear?" He left the room.

Bethia sat by the window for a long time, dabbing at her tears.

MARYETTA WAS COMING from her grandfather's workshop when she heard the sound of the wagon rumbling up the driveway. She ran toward it, smiling and flushed at seeing Matthew.

"You didn't bring me flowers!" she exclaimed in mock disappointment, slipping her arm through his. "Wait here. I'll tell Trudy we shall be back in a short while."

When she returned, they walked in the direction of the pond and Maryetta chattered away about the wedding plans. She stopped when they were beyond sight of her grandparents and looked at Matthew.

"I've watched for you every day—I thought you'd never come. You must be very busy."

Her arms, cool and soft, stole around his neck and she lifted her face to his.

Matthew kissed her—how could he not?

When they resumed their walk, Maryetta began to sense that all was not well.

"Are you troubled about something?" she asked, never dreaming what was in store.

Matthew's answer came slowly, hesitantly. "I have been

thinking—perhaps we were premature—"

Maryetta froze. The hunted animal look crept back into the gray eyes.

"What I mean is—I really didn't give you a chance. There are others, you know—others who have far more to offer you than I."

"But I don't love any other—and I have never cared what they had to offer!" Maryetta felt the quick, hot tears flooding her eyes and struggled against them.

"You would never have to worry about being cold with someone like—Isaac Timens."

"Matthew Haddon! If you have decided you don't want me, say so!"

Matthew walked away, but Maryetta followed him. Scenes of the past clicked in her memory with kaleidoscope clarity—the wooden barrier that had denied her her mother's arms—the water of New York harbor stretching wider and wider, with her father and Ellen fading from sight—the strips of cloth nailed over Sister Celeste's door. Was it always to be this way? The abandonment—the stripping away of everything she wanted?

She stepped in front of Matthew, her tears now unchecked and running down her face.

"If this is how you really feel—" She stopped and swallowed, tasting salt and hating her weakness. "If this is what you really want, perhaps I will see others. Perhaps I will see lots of others—even Isaac Timens." And she turned and ran toward the house.

Matthew heard the door shut and stood looking miserable. How could he possibly have told her he had lost his job—had no income and no future left in the little city? It was true, if she married Timens she would never have to want for anything. How could he compete with that?

But the thought of Maryetta in another man's arms sent madness to his brain. He stamped back up the path, climbed aboard the old wagon, and whipped the startled Dandy down the steep incline and out onto the dusty road.

MARYETTA STOOD AT THE WINDOW and watched the wagon depart. She was glad Grandpa Downing was out working on his cabinets. But Trudy was there, and the older woman reached a comforting arm around her without questioning or saying a word.

"What is wrong with me, Grandma? Why doesn't anyone want me? Why is it always like this? Why won't God let me have anyone?"

"You have us, Maryetta—your grandpa and me. You know we want you."

But Maryetta was beyond reason.

"But you could change—even you could change!"

"Maryetta, talk sense."

"I don't know what's sensible! I really don't know!" Maryetta fled to her room and closed the door behind her.

A month went by, and Maryetta kept to herself, clothing herself in an impenetrable armor that forbade conversation. When she did speak, it was impersonally.

The rejection by Matthew was one thing, but the added knowledge that her friendship with Bethia could end was another. She would have to see Bethia soon to know where she stood with Matthew's sister. She wrote her a letter and set a date to see her when her grandparents were in Newburyport.

IT WAS THE END OF JUNE when the two finally met, and the occasion was awkward for both.

"I've always loved the smell of ice-cream parlors," Bethia said lightly as they settled into metal chairs with heart-shaped backs. "It's like ice and vanilla."

Maryetta didn't smile. It was evident that thoughts of ice and vanilla were far from her mind. Instead she was studying Bethia.

"How much do you know about Matthew and me?" she asked bluntly.

Bethia shrank from this new Maryetta—cold, impersonal. Nor

did she like the deceptive role she was forced to assume, knowing that she must heed her brother's directive to stay out of his affairs.

"Only that he never looked at a girl until you came along," she answered cautiously.

"He asked me to marry him. Did you know that? And then he changed his mind. I'd like to know why."

"If you knew Matthew, you would know that he never does anything without a logical reason."

Bethia hated the situation—defending and protecting her brother when she believed he was wrong. She could see her friend's pain, see that she was striving to keep back the tears.

"He never said why—I can only guess. He must have seen something in me that he didn't like. I have been doing as he suggested and seeing Isaac Timens. So far he hasn't discovered how awful I am."

"Oh, Maryetta!" Bethia exclaimed. "There is nothing awful about you! Don't even think such a thing!"

"You are still my friend?"

"Of course I am still your friend. How could you think otherwise?"

"I don't know. I guess it is just the way my life seems to go."

"Well, I am your friend and always shall be."

Maryetta smiled for the first time. The smile removed all pretense.

"Isaac has asked me to marry him," she confided. "He has always been quite ardent—ever since he was my pupil."

Bethia couldn't hide her dismay. "You haven't said you would?"

"No. I have put him off until I return from seeing my father."

"You aren't allowing yourself any time, Maryetta."

But Maryetta was talking fast. "I am going to New York, Bethia. I must get some things settled. But I need to ask a favor. My grandparents cannot meet me at the train when I return; they had made plans to be in New Hampshire before I purchased my fare. Do you think you could meet me and take me back to

Byfield? I'd pay you."

"Of course I will meet you—and not at a cost."

"I have another favor."

Bethia waited.

"I shall need your prayers. I do not know what to expect, and I am so full of anger—and fear!"

"Anger isn't good, Maryetta. Neither is fear. Father taught us to leave such things at the Cross."

"But you do not know how cruel my parents have been."

The perceptive Bethia studied her friend.

"You are letting bitterness rule your life, Maryetta. You must let Jesus help you overcome that."

"Someday, perhaps—but not now," Maryetta answered. "My father has got to know the truth, and I intend to tell him."

"Very well, but I've a feeling you have the cart before the horse."

Maryetta was getting to her feet. "I leave in a week—July 7. I will be back on the afternoon train on July 10."

Bethia watched Maryetta leave, and a frown creased her usually placid brow. *I don't believe Maryetta has ever given any part of her life to You, Jesus. How she needs to experience Your peace!*

19

The projected journey proceeded without incident. In Boston, Maryetta changed trains and boarded the New York Traveler. By the time she had arrived in the Empire State she was tired, stiff, and feeling the oppression of the gray and murky atmosphere so common to big cities when night moves into dawn. It was the same terrible inertia and nausea she had felt as an eight year old when Lydia had dressed her for the channel crossing.

Resentment stirred afresh toward her stepmother. She checked the address again, the one Ellen had given her, and was soon entering the lobby of the city's finest hotel. It was apparent that the Ira Cobbets enjoyed a lifestyle vastly different from her own. Stopping at the desk, she wrote out a note and sent it ahead of her, then began to climb the green carpeted stairway.

Trembling, and with her young heart beating madly, Maryetta knocked at the designated door. A uniformed man opened it and ushered her inside to a plush waiting room. Maryetta was not its only occupant; a young auburn-haired girl was also waiting.

At first they sat in silence while the minutes ticked off, then uneasily they entered into a conversation.

"Does she do this purposely—make us wait?" asked the girl.

Maryetta shrugged her shoulders, feeling the old helplessness Lydia had always engendered.

"Maybe I should not have come. I'm told she's a dreadful employer."

"You are applying for work?" asked Maryetta.

"Yes, aren't you?"

A door opened before Maryetta could reply, and the same servant who had ushered her into the waiting room beckoned for her to follow.

Down a dark hallway and into a spacious room walked Maryetta. The heavy hangings at the windows were meant to be imperious, but to Maryetta they were only shutting out the daylight. A fracture where the draperies met let a narrow streak of light through, and it had stolen its way to a huge ornate mirror and targeted Maryetta, blinding her for a moment. When she could see, she became aware of the heavy, cumbersome furnishings, all belonging to another age, another culture—the miserable world of a proud and hateful woman.

"Oh, Lord!" breathed Maryetta. "I should die in such oppression."

Something stirred in the shadows, and Maryetta saw that there was a woman seated behind a block-style mahogany desk. Lydia Cobbet sat like a haughty bejeweled empress posing for a state portrait. As always, she was overdressed. Her sharp, censoring eyes appraised Maryetta.

Maryetta stared, hoping to see something of kindness, something of humility, but as always the eyes were of steel—unfathomable, never betraying what was going on behind them. Still there was something different, something Maryetta had never noticed before. Could it be the deep lines that etched the once flawless complexion, or the dark shadows that discolored the lids? the flabby jowls and neck lines that bespoke age? Yet Lydia was not that old!

The alteration both shocked and stirred a latent sympathy within her. But she had not come prepared to feel sorry for her enemy; she had come to get even—to pay back this evil woman for the years of denial forced upon her. Her thoughts were interrupted by the familiar harsh voice.

"So! Maryetta has come home!"

The hard tone, acrimonious and unfeeling, sent a chill through Maryetta. She breathed deeply. What she had come to say, she would say.

"No, Lydia. If you think I am here to stay, you are mistaken. I do not force myself upon those who do not want me. I have come only to see my father."

Lydia arose unsteadily and crossed to the window where the shaft of light had intruded. There was an unmistakable slump to her shoulders and a much-too-early widow's hump deforming what Maryetta remembered as a very shapely back.

"I am afraid that will be impossible," Lydia said without emotion.

Maryetta felt the anger rising, stifling her. It was an anger that could kill if given the opportunity.

"Why impossible? Isn't he here?"

"No!" Lydia took a deep breath. "I buried him several weeks ago—in Washington, D.C." As the older woman spoke, she turned. "I am sorry. I am truly sorry." Her lips trembled.

Ashen now and shaking uncontrollably, Maryetta tried desperately to gain some composure. But the words had found their mark, and suddenly she burst into tears and sobbed as though her heart would break. She covered her eyes with gloved hands and felt the hot tears through their mesh.

Lydia had triumphed again—had succeeded in delivering her own brand of a *coup de grâce.*

When Maryetta could find her voice, she spoke without feeling.

"I see. I see I have made a mistake . . . a miserable mistake . . . ever thinking, ever hoping. You have won again, Lydia . . . taken everything from me . . . but I shall never know why you have hated me so."

She turned and started for the door. Halfway there, she heard Lydia's hurried step behind her and felt a restraining hand on her shoulder.

"Wait—don't go. I want to talk to you."

Maryetta turned toward her tormentor. "Talk to me? Haven't you said enough? What kind of person are you? What pleasure do you get from taking the heart out of people?" Maryetta never wanted to see the woman again.

Then she saw tears on the tired face, and curiosity arrested her. In the months that she had lived with Lydia, she had never seen her cry; she had not believed her stepmother capable of any feeling. Suddenly weak and uncertain, she allowed herself to be led to a short sofa.

Lydia began to speak rapidly, as though she must complete her sentences while she had Maryetta within hearing.

"I want you to know that I am sorry—terribly sorry for the years of grief I caused you—and your father. For years I deliberately separated you. I confess, I worked hard at it. I was determined to have him to myself. I couldn't bear to share his love with anyone!"

Maryetta stared, disbelief clouding her features. What kind of a nightmare was this? This artful woman stripped of her dignity, admitting her selfishness.

Lydia went on. "He was a good man, Maryetta. He hated contention. I wish now that he had not gone along with me, because I watched his love for me turn into endurance. He found his peace only in his work and went to California more and more. There he could lose himself, build some respect—and get away from me! I became less and less a part of his life.

"So you see, what I denied you, I denied myself. I did love him—selfishly, with a destructive kind of love. I don't expect that you can understand or forgive me.

"I told him that I had lied about your stealing my brooch. He said he had never believed me, and that he had sent you away to protect you from me. What do you think of that?"

A strange light began to dawn on Maryetta as she looked at the miserable woman facing her. Lydia, once so very beautiful, was now broken and bearing the marks of guilt, age, and the loneliness she had foisted upon others.

This woman was no victor—she was a pitiful vanquished enemy, and Maryetta had had no hand in her defeat. Had not Sister Celeste told her how useless was her desire to repay? Had she not said "pray" and "forgive"? Now Lydia was pleading and tearful, needing to know that she was not altogether worthless.

"I appear complete, very comfortable, do I not? Needing nothing? Well, let me tell you, all that one sees simply is not there. There is no satisfaction in things—no family, no love, nor friends. In my position, one can never know the real from the false, the true from the hypocrite. One can grow distrusting and—bitter."

Strange that Lydia should use that word, that convicting word. Maryetta knew something of bitterness. Had it not dogged every phase of her young life? Had not her very best friends seen it growing in her and warned her of its poison?

And this brokenness! This she had never anticipated! She had never seen Lydia as the loser—the poverty-stricken one needing all that God in His grace had blessed upon her own life. The love of Ellen, the precious unassuming convent sisters, Celeste, the Goettes, Nigel Edmunds, the sweetness of Janine, Antoinette, and Louise—and all the while, the heavenly Bridegroom had been patiently overlooking her hard heart and drawing her to Himself—meeting every need as she faced it.

How mistaken and how blind she had been to entertain the real enemy—the joy killer. *Oh, Mara—you are indeed a robber, and I am a hopeless sinner, taking for granted the kindness of God—not wanting Him! Wanting everything my way. Forgive me, gentle Savior—please forgive me and fill me with Yourself.*

Lydia had walked to the dark window and pulled the cord, allowing the sunlight to stream in. With it peace, too, swept in upon Maryetta, a peace that nothing could destroy—not even her father's death, not even Matthew's rejection. This was a holy peace, born of an alliance with Jesus Christ. To think that she might have had it years ago when Nigel Edmunds had suggested it. . . .

How absurd that here, in the house of her enemy, she was receiving God's forgiveness and His strength and new life. She should have been at a church altar—perhaps on her knees beside a convent bed—but never in this room.

Yes, Mara had had to die before Maryetta could live—and it was plain to Maryetta that she herself had to die too. Oh, the mystery of Christ!

God was "manifest in the flesh, justified in the spirit, seen of angels, preached unto the Gentiles, believed on in the world, received up into glory." The words she had been reading, that had seemed to mean nothing, now came to her with astounding clarity, blessing her soul and causing her to see Lydia as she had never seen her—and to see a God she had never understood!

"Oh." Maryetta breathed a long sigh. "Oh—I am so rich," she murmured.

"What did you say?"

Lydia's question brought Maryetta back to the moment with a start.

"I said I am rich, Lydia—truly rich! It was all meant for evil—but God meant it for good."

Lydia clearly did not have any idea what Maryetta was talking about. But, "Stay and have dinner with me, Maryetta," she entreated. "You can tell me about Europe—did you ever see the King of Belgium and his family?"

Sympathy flooded Maryetta's heart. Poor Lydia, still so taken up with her royalty worship—what a pity that that was all she really had. Perhaps someday she could show her another way—but right now she was so new in Christ—just feeling her own guilt roll off her back. . . .

She looked at the pleading woman. "I will stay, Lydia," she said.

"Truly, Maryetta, you are quite beautiful. I would give anything if your father might have seen you."

After dinner, Maryetta accepted Lydia's invitation to stay for a night or more. She could see that her stepmother was making an effort to erase the memories of their early years. But Maryetta knew where she would be spending the rest of her life. She had a place in New England where she had been taken in and shown the love she had always coveted, and she knew that would always be her home.

And what a relief to know she was now in a partnership with the Lord of creation, that she could enter into an intimacy she had always wanted with God. She could trust the future—the "expected end" Trudy had talked about—to the One who had loved her enough to die for her sins and bring her to God.

MARYETTA'S TRAIN entered the Boston yards on July 10 as she had planned. In no time she was boarding the train for Newburyport and home. She marveled at the joy that was flooding her soul. Everything that had looked so gloomy before had changed drastically.

The brakeman opened the end door of the car and bellowed in his usual way. Maryetta recalled how on her first trip she had been so startled with the strange ways of the Americans—and remembered too how she had looked into the eyes of the handsome stranger across the aisle.

Somehow, she could now feel sorry for Matthew, could even pray for him—but for some reason she could not think of him as she once had. And Isaac Timens—of course she could never settle down with a marriage of convenience, and she would tell him so as soon as possible.

She stepped down onto the Newburyport platform and searched the sloping street for Bethia. Bethia, the precious friend who had told her she had the cart before the horse—Maryetta could hardly wait to tell her all that had happened.

But the perceptive Bethia needed no explanation. She could see that this was not the same vindictive, cold creature she had watched board the train three days ago.

"Your visit was a good one, I can see," said Bethia, helping

Maryetta into the wagon.

"I shall tell you all about it someday. Right now I can't wait to let my grandparents know how much I love them."

Bethia was smiling.

"And how is Matthew?" asked Maryetta, surprising Bethia with so casual an inquiry.

"He manages to appear all right, though he has gone back to D.C."

Maryetta sighed wistfully. "I didn't think he would want to put that much distance between us."

Bethia felt free now to speak up.

"I told him to talk it out with you, but you know Matthew. He trusts nothing to love or to God's grace. He always makes his decisions with such a practical viewpoint."

"What will he do in Washington?"

"He has gone back to editing. He said he had to make a new start in a less-complicated environment. I am guessing he was made a good offer. He seems to have a reputation in the Capitol."

"Can you tell me now why he changed as he did?"

Bethia was slow to reply, but this new Maryetta was easy to talk to.

"It wasn't you, Maryetta. It was the same old bugaboo that has always plagued Matthew—he lacks confidence. He was once eased out of West Point after getting his nomination and qualifying scholastically. I don't believe he ever got over it. He lost his position with the paper. He wanted so very much to impress you."

Maryetta looked pensive. "I think I can understand. I saw that in him when he came to my classes."

They rode along in silence until Bethia spoke again. "What will you do now, Maryetta?"

"Oh, doubtless go on with my French classes."

Bethia brightened. "You'll stay with your grandparents?"

"Yes, for a while. They are my family—my own dear family. But I do wish their home was better weather-proofed—the winters in Byfield are dreadful!"

Bethia reached a warm hand over Maryetta's. "Well, that means we shall see one another often, I hope."

Maryetta looked pleased. "I would welcome that," she said.

20

When Maryetta resumed her French classes, she was once again overwhelmed with the numbers that flocked to her door. The summer days were proving profitable and satisfying. There was enough money to pay her grandparents a small board and she was able to purchase yardage to improve her wardrobe, besides. She looked forward to the autumn when she could help Trudy with the canning and the storing in of the last crops.

Very early one Monday morning she heard wagon wheels on the gravel of the steep driveway and went to the side door. She watched as Bethia climbed down, tethered her horse, and came toward her smiling.

"This is probably one of our last warm days, Maryetta. We have decided we should take advantage of it and go to the island. I thought you would like to go too."

Maryetta stood with a doubtful expression on her face, wondering how many members of Matthew's family knew of their broken relationship.

The discerning Bethia was quick to read her friend's thoughts.

"Don't be concerned about the family. They all know how private a person Matthew is. He shares very little information with his family."

That was not enough for Maryetta.

"I promised Trudy I would help with the preserving," she protested.

"Oh, Maryetta, you can always work. You must have a little fun! Have you ever been to a clambake? Of course you haven't!"

Maryetta savored the pleasant thought of a day without a demanding schedule.

"I will go if Trudy says I might," she said.

Grandma Trudy was as anxious as Bethia to see Maryetta take a day off. In no time the two friends, with Dandy trotting joyfully, were off for a day at Plum Island.

When Bethia and Maryetta arrived, they found that the entire Haddon family had preceded them. Already Clinton had set up a tent and was digging a trench with the help of Drake and Joshua. Caroline and her family were there, and little Elise ran up and down the grassy sand dunes, the sun reflecting off her galvanized sand pail. Cousin Allen, Clara, and Phoebe were there, also, and Phoebe's new husband.

Maryetta was received as warmly as any of the family and quickly joined the others in their frolic. The morning passed quickly under the pleasant sun and in the splashing waves. Maryetta took time to admire Elise's plunder of dead crabs, live minnows, seaweed, and shells. By afternoon the men were filling the trench with large stones and starting a fire. Maryetta watched entranced as the fires were raked out and replaced with buckets full of clams and lobsters.

The women added small potatoes and corn and helped to cover it all with seaweed. Phoebe made much ado about melting butter from Clinton's dairy and adding her own homemade vinegar to it. Her drawn butter sauce was her special contribution!

The Plum Island dinnerware of cracked and discolored old dishes was passed around, and in no time the family had gathered in a circle to await the doling out of New England's favorite foods.

Elise came and settled at Maryetta's feet, where she took great delight in showing her how to open the clams and remove the black veil from their heads. For some reason there seemed to be a bonding affection between Caroline's small child and Maryetta. Perhaps it was the belief in Maryetta's heart that she would never have a child—or perhaps it was the child within her that had always wanted more family. At any rate, there was a drawing to one another that satisfied them both.

When the sun began to sink and the fires were replenished, they gathered together and began to sing. Clinton had not enough light to read the Bible, but he had enough vigor to lead them in a vesper hymn. Elise cuddled against Maryetta's breast and the fires painted each face with a golden glow as they joined in song.

Maryetta scanned the heavens, by now studded with twinkling gemlike stars. She thought about King David of old, how as a young boy he must have sat under the same canopied sky and set to music his own songs of praise. From the depths of his being he had communicated with God, and God with him, and ultimately he had given to the world a wealth of psalms, all replete with God's wisdom, praise, blessing, and comfort.

How many altars of praise had been raised over the centuries? How many tongues had gladdened the heart of God? And the miracle of it all—that someday, as one of His little sheep, she would know. The thought was overwhelming!

Maryetta found herself back in the convent, listening to the nuns as they sang a final night song when the lighted candles had been quenched. One holy family, one heavenly flame of devotion, one flock—that was what the Savior had prayed in His last hours. Oh, the longing to see the walls that men had erected torn down! Oh, that the blood-bought children in all camps could be one—no ill will, no division, just believers seeking the face of Jesus!

When it grew late, the packing of gear began. It seemed a shame to leave such a loving group and heavenly day behind. Jerome came for his sleeping daughter and thanked Maryetta for caring for her.

"She has never gone to anyone the way she has gone to you," he said.

That pleased Maryetta, but embarrassed her too, and she quickly changed the subject.

"You are enjoying your sabbatical from the concert stage."

"I have never enjoyed anything more. Family life should definitely be a priority!"

Joshua drove on the way home, and Bethia and Maryetta bedded down in the back of the wagon. Allen and the others left in his wagon. A gigantic moon had risen, all deep yellow and full, and a balmy evening breeze licked at Maryetta's sunburned face and arms.

Surely with the coming of new life, there had come also blessings Maryetta could never have imagined. It seemed that the Lord was opening the windows of heaven and pouring down everything good. Surely there could be no more to desire.

WHEN MARYETTA AWOKE the next morning, she found a brown envelope beside her dish on the breakfast table. As was usual, her grandparents were early in the fields.

Grandfather must have brought this from the local post office while I was at Plum Island, she mused, opening the envelope with mild interest. The New York address meant nothing to her.

By the time she had read the first few lines, her eyes had widened and she was on her feet, shaking and gasping. When she recovered her breath, she raced into the fields, madly waving the letter.

"Grandfather! Grandma Trudy! You won't believe it!"

Stumbling and laughing, she covered the rough ground quickly and stood dumbfounded before them.

"Well, read it to us, Maryetta!" said Grandfather impatiently.

Swallowing and gaining some composure, she read the astounding news aloud.

To Maryetta Cobbet:

I have been employed to apprise you of the following bequest as stated in your father's last will and testament. Within a few days you may be expecting a bank draft for $5,000, the amount *designated by your father. Please contact me if you have any questions or if you do not receive the draft within a few days.*

Very truly yours,
John K. Church
Attorney-at-Law

When Maryetta finished, Grandma Trudy stood with a satisfied grin.

"Well, my little orphan, it seems God's thoughts are on you in full measure. I always did believe your day would come."

Grandfather was not as charitable.

"Tain't half what he owed you for the grief he caused you," he commented tacitly.

"Oh, but Grandfather! Now I can have my own business!"

"Well, we'll see."

And though he tried not to show it, Maryetta knew her grandfather was as pleased and relieved as she that, even in a remote and unexpected way, Dr. Ira Cobbet had at last assured his daughter that he had not forgotten her.

When the promised bank draft arrived, Grandfather Downing drove the bays down the turnpike where Maryetta opened her first account at the Port city's bank. It was a gala event for them all. Later he drove Maryetta out to the Haddon farm, for she could hardly wait to tell her friend of her good fortune.

She read her treasured letter to an open-mouthed Bethia.

"Gracious! Whatever will you do with a fortune?" Bethia exclaimed.

"Five thousand dollars isn't really a fortune, Bethia."

Bethia whistled. "You'll be rich. You'll travel and dress like a princess, and you'll forget all your old friends!"

Maryetta shivered. Bethia was bringing to mind Lydia and her misplaced affections.

"Never, Bethia. Never! I have seen what greed for power and money can do to a person."

"Then you will stay at your grandpa's?"

A gentle soft smile played at the corners of Maryetta's mouth.

"I shall always live close to them. They are my family, and I shall cast my lot with the people who truly love me. But I would really like to have a place of my own. Nothing elaborate—just a very little house in Newburyport that I can heat easily. I'd like to start a dressmaking business of my own."

"Won't your grandfather object to your leaving?"

"I won't be going very far. Besides, I think Grandpa and Grandma Trudy have had a guest long enough. I don't think they'll object to being by themselves again."

"But you would not like living alone, would you?"

Maryetta was still smiling. "I will not be living alone."

Bethia raised her eyebrows in question.

"You are right, Bethia. I would not like living alone—not one bit. I think I shall be making some very special plans—for a very special person to join me!"

"Your Ellen!" exclaimed the perceptive Bethia, delighted with the thought. "What a perfect plan!"

21

October introduced herself with brisk and nippy winds, but still had a beauty all her own. Once again early frosts were touching the foliage with riotous colors and sending wonder to Maryetta's gray eyes.

Bethia accepted her invitation to join in the hunt for a house. The two friends chattered amiably as they walked the leaf-strewn sidewalks and stopped to pick up the fallen mahogany chestnuts. They came to a narrow lane leading off of Atwood Street, where the houses were small and boasted little yard—in fact, they seemed to grow right out of the dirt sidewalk.

Maryetta was quick to see a sign posted by the door of one little dwelling.

"Do you really want to buy a salt-box?" asked Bethia.

"I could heat it—and it is close to town."

Maryetta could see that it was a good location for her dressmaking plans.

"It needs paint," commented Bethia.

"I've enough money for that."

"And we all would help—Joshua, Papa, Allen, and Drake!"

Maryetta caught the wistfulness in Bethia's expression when she spoke that last name.

"Tell me about Drake," she said.

Bethia blushed.

"You like that man, don't you?"

Bethia still demurred.

"That's all right," said Maryetta. "You needn't say if you don't want to."

That seemed to loosen Bethia's tongue. "You know he was badly wounded in the war."

"Yes, I have noticed that he has difficulty walking."

Bethia sighed. "He thinks that everyone notices."

"One can scarcely avoid it."

"I don't ever see it," said Bethia. "I see only that he is a very beautiful person . . . good to be with . . . kind."

"Does he know that you see him like that?"

"He doesn't want to. And he'd never consider marriage. He told father that he could never burden a woman with half a man. I think he is resigned to being a bachelor for ever."

"Well, now we have something we can pray about—together!"

Maryetta lost no time looking up the owner of the salt-box, and soon they were working out the details for a transfer of ownership.

The Haddons came often with their paint brushes, hammers, nails, and putty. Grandpa and Grandma Trudy brought enough pine and oak to keep the fires blazing all winter. And that was not all. Grandpa came one day with a wagon full of gifts and a pleased look on his face. He had made his granddaughter one of his exquisite desks and a number of small tables.

"I have never owned anything before!" exclaimed Maryetta, adding the last touch to the ruffled curtains in the sitting room. "Isn't it fun?"

By the end of October, she had moved in and was working diligently on her spare bedroom. She scrubbed the old fireplaces and stacked logs beside them, varnished woodwork, and spent long hours at her new sewing machine. She bought pretty pictures and clocks and even a piano.

Then one afternoon she pressed Joshua and Bethia to take her to the incoming Boston train. They pulled the wagon in behind the train station where they might watch as the passengers arrived. The iron monster trumpeted its arrival before coming around the bend and was fast approaching the open iron doors and setting off the clamoring bells.

All three got down from the wagon and made their way to the platform where the train had come to a steamy halt. Passengers stepped down and quickly dispersed, each going in his own direction—except for one little old lady who stood looking bewildered. She wore a very large black hat, very much out of style. In one hand she clutched a worn purse, as out-of-date as the hat, and in the other hand she held tight to a battered old suitcase.

Bethia broke into a characteristic grin. "That must be your Ellen!" she exclaimed.

Joshua and Bethia hung back and watched as Maryetta hugged and kissed her old nurse. With their arms still around each other, Maryetta introduced Ellen to her friends, all the while dabbing away at tears of joy.

They boarded the wagon and took off, with Ellen, now along in years, as skittish about this mode of travel as Maryetta had been at the first. When they opened the door to the little renovated salt-box, there was an unexpected surprise awaiting Maryetta and her guest. The house was teaming with Haddons and Downings. Delightful fragrances came from pots and pans boiling on the stove, and every fireplace was ablaze with welcome!

Of course, when Ellen was shown her bedroom, it was a time for more tears and laughter. The day ended with promises of many winter reunions.

Maryetta added more logs to the fire and sat down with Ellen beside the crackling logs—life replete and thankfulness flooding her heart.

"You shall never have to move again, Ellen. You shall be my very own mother, and we shall be together forever."

"If only I could have brought Tishme," said Ellen.

"Whatever happened to Tishme?"

"Y'won't believe it if I tell you. She died of a bee sting!"

Maryetta couldn't help herself. She laughed. "Oh, Ellen, she was such an incorrigible! She never did learn!"

THE HOUSE, so close to town, proved an excellent location for Maryetta's new venture, and it did not take long for Mrs. Stuart's patrons to discover the new address of the European stylist.

Winter came early, with its spasmodic snowstorms, but the little house met all of Maryetta's expectations. It remained cozy and warm on the coldest of days.

The Haddons visited often, and many an evening Clinton taught from his Bible. Together they closed their evenings with a hymn of praise around the piano. Sometimes Caroline and Jerome came, too, much to the delight of little Elise, who by now had claimed Maryetta for her own.

"What do you hear from Matthew?" Maryetta asked one night, glad that she could speak of him without bitterness.

"I believe he is finding himself," answered Caroline. "He is rising rapidly in his chosen field. He expects to purchase his own paper soon."

"And he won't come home again?"

"That I doubt, but I plan to visit him. Perhaps I can persuade him to return and start his own newspaper here."

"If anyone can, it is Carrie," said Jerome. "He listens to her."

22

Maryetta had never been happier, and it seemed truly to be a time for the "singing of birds." She had managed her money well and was living comfortably. When weather permitted, she and Ellen spent pleasant times at the Haddon farm.

On one such an occasion the family was celebrating Joshua's birthday. It surprised Maryetta to find Jerome and Elise there without their wife and mother.

"Where is Caroline?" she asked Bethia.

"She has gone to Washington to see Matthew."

"She still hopes he will come back!"

"Yes. She is expected home in another day, maybe two, and then we will know."

When the clock struck nine, Maryetta arose and Ellen with her.

"Busy day tomorrow—we must go."

Joshua left for the barn and set about harnessing Dandy to the wagon. He hung a lighted lantern on the side of the wagon and escorted the two ladies through the side door. They climbed aboard and were settling in their seats when they heard the pounding of hooves on the muddy road.

"Someone's really pushing his horse—and at a late hour," observed the youngest Haddon. He waited to see who it could be.

The rider was Whitey Holcomb, a man the Haddons knew from the telegraph office. From what they could see in the darkness, he was distraught and disheveled.

"A message for Clinton Haddon," announced the breathless rider, his voice raucous in the stillness of the night. It seemed as though a dark angel had made its appearance from the environs of hell.

Clinton stepped out from the door. "Right here," he announced.

"It's bad news, sir. I'm sorry."

The rider handed Clinton a piece of paper, turned his horse about, and vanished into the darkness whence he had come.

Clinton walked back to the house where he had light enough to read by. Maryetta and the others clustered about, waiting to hear what message the paper contained.

The usually placid Clinton gave a gasp, and a tremor seemed to roll over him like an earthquake. Then he tried to steady himself. It was all in his face—the shock, the need to go from where he was to where he must act.

"Father, what is it?" asked the stricken Bethia.

Clinton stood transfixed and silent. He made an effort to speak and stopped, seeming to have no breath. Bethia took the paper from his hand.

"Oh, no! No, it cannot be. Father, Jerome—it's Caroline!"

Stunned and pale faced, Jerome took the message from her and read it. "There must be a mistake! When is the next train out?"

Maryetta and Ellen stood wondering, and Bethia stumbled toward them, but Drake interposed and steadied her in his arms.

"There has been a train wreck," Bethia managed. "On the New York line. They found Caroline's purse—but not Caroline."

"She is injured?" whispered Maryetta.

"They haven't found her!" repeated Bethia through her sobs.

The words struck with the stunning paralysis of lightning. Clinton, Jerome, and Joshua immediately climbed into the wagon and headed toward town.

Knowing what devastation would be put upon the family if worse news came, Maryetta moved to pacify the frightened Elise.

"Would you like to come visit me, Elise, till your daddy gets back?"

Elise went to her friend immediately, and Maryetta swept the child up into her arms.

"I'll get Allen," said Bethia. "He will take you home."

Clinton and Jerome caught the stage just as it was emerging from Thread-Needle Alley. They traveled through the night, arriving in Boston in time to get a train for New Haven, where the telegram had said the injured passengers had been taken. The Boston newspapers were already on the street, carrying the gruesome account of the train wreck. Clinton bought one as they boarded the train for New Haven.

It seemed that the ill-fated train had been coming around a curve at full speed, passing through a dynamited ledge. A defect in one of the sleepers had caused the rail to give way and the entire train to derail. The engine and tender, well loaded with fuel and water, had broken from the cars, and the cars had jammed into the ledge, smashing to kindling! It was from this wreckage that the dead and injured had been conveyed to a nearby field.

A surgeon, who himself had escaped injury, was cited for bravery and courage for spending the night administering medical help to the hapless travelers. An oncoming train had been flagged down several miles from the wreckage and its crew sent to help. Within hours, the casualties had been transported to New Haven.

Clinton passed the paper to Jerome, who refused it. Clinton, who had been through the worst of the battles in the War between the States, had never seen anyone in such a state of shock as his son-in-law.

The city of New Haven was no stranger to Clinton. He had not only spent months there recuperating from his battle wounds, but it was there that he had spent the night with his dying brother.

A shudder passed over his large frame as they entered the hospital door and painful memories flooded through him. There was much activity, a feeling of urgency with nurses, doctors, and attendants hurrying through the old halls.

"We have come about my daughter," said Clinton to the woman at the desk.

"Name, please."

"Caroline Cavell."

The woman scanned a sheet of paper. "She is not here."

Clinton could feel Jerome stiffen at his side.

"There are other hospitals," he said, hoping to encourage him.

But at each hospital the answer was the same.

"There is only one more place to look," said Clinton, desperation now marking his own features.

Jerome nodded and turned even paler.

They went to two undertaking establishments and then wearily climbed the stairs to a third. Yes, there were several unidentified victims.

"Stay here, Jerome. I will check them out," said Clinton.

When he returned, he didn't have to speak—nor could he. Jerome read the message in his father-in-law's face.

"Where is she?" His voice was as dull and dolorous as his surroundings.

"I'll take you to her."

The two entered a dimly lit room and approached a rudely made gurney, where lay the silent form of their beautiful Caroline. They could see that she had been struck a deadly blow on the head, but otherwise she looked the same—as lovely as ever and peacefully asleep.

Jerome touched her head where blood had dried in her hair and ran a hand gently over the wound.

"She was hurt, Clinton—and I wasn't there."

Clinton waited for Jerome to break—wished that he would break. It wasn't natural.

"I wasn't there," he kept repeating.

"Come, we must make arrangements to take her home," said Clinton.

"No. I won't leave her alone again," was the stubborn answer.

Clinton did not argue. Perhaps this was Jerome's way of grieving. He would leave him to handle his pain in his own way.

GRIEF FOR THE HADDON FAMILY had never been more real. To have lost their beloved Caroline at so young an age was something they could neither comprehend nor bear. Maryetta spent most of her hours at the farm, taking over many tasks and bolstering their spirits, but never penetrating their tearful daze. Ellen had taken Elise under her care where she might be spared the sight of her grieving family.

Each night Maryetta returned to her little house and made an effort to prepare the little one for a life without her mother. She talked of heaven's beauties and the Savior's mansions and how Caroline had gone to visit the place.

Jerome came to her door the day of the funeral to get his daughter.

"I have to bring Elise to the house, to say good-bye to her mother," he began.

The statement brought Maryetta up rigid. Carved deeply in her memory was the day she had been taken into her own mother's bedroom to "say good-bye." She had to speak up. Stepping between Jerome and Elise, she said, "Are you certain that is what you want to do?"

Jerome looked at her curiously.

"Please, Mr. Cavell, give it some thought."

"But, of course—I have."

"No. If you had, you would not take her to a mother who cannot respond. Please don't."

"But I must."

"Oh, Mr. Cavell, you cannot leave her with the dreadful memory of a mother who will look so foreign to her. Let her remember her as she was in life—"

"I don't understand."

"But I do! My father made me say good-bye to my mother when I was the same age as Elise. She was just a shadow of her real self, and the memory has never left me! Please don't do that to Elise!"

Jerome groped through the shadows that encompassed him, seeking to reason. It was obvious that this girl was opposing him for a reason, but he lacked the energy to deal with it. He looked down at his shoes in resignation.

"Very well," he said and took his leave.

Maryetta looked after him, her eyes overflowing with tears. She wanted desperately to take away the grief he was feeling, wanted to comfort him—but it was no use. He would have to grow out of his grief as she had done.

THE WINTER MOVED ON, and Maryetta continued to make time for the Haddons. Matthew had not come home for the funeral. It was evident that he had severed all relationship with his family. Perhaps he felt responsible for Caroline's death, since she had been traveling to see him. In any case, it was clear to Maryetta that he intended to stay away from bad memories.

Gradually she could see that the business of living was helping the rest of the family begin to get over their loss—except for Jerome. He had cut himself off from even his music, and several times Clinton had found him at Caroline's grave—still without tears.

"Jerome has us worried, Maryetta," confided Bethia. "He speaks often of dying. He is bringing Elise to us tomorrow—says she wants to come and he can't blame her. The house is terribly empty with only two servants to meet her needs."

Maryetta recalled how lonely the little Iowa cabin had seemed after her mother died.

"Would you ask Jerome to come and see me?" asked Maryetta.

"He isn't very responsive to suggestions."

But the next day her doorbell rang, and Maryetta found Jerome Cavell on her front step, holding Elise by the hand.

"Bethia said you wanted to see me."

Elise slipped her hand from his grasp and ran to the kitchen to visit with Ellen.

"Come in," said Maryetta, making a concentrated effort to hide her shock at Jerome's appearance. He was thin and haggard, his skin sallow and darkly shadowed around his eyes—she never could have imagined the svelte Jerome Cavell dressed as carelessly as the man now facing her.

Maryetta went straight to the point. "You aren't adjusting."

"Does one ever?" he asked.

"The passing of time does help."

"How much time? The memories don't go away."

"Someday you will be glad for the memories."

"They eat me up . . . and I can think of only one way to stop them."

"But it isn't God's way."

The pain and the hurt in Jerome's eyes rivaled Maryetta's determination to shock him into seeing his error, but she could not stop now. He was looking at her with a flash of anger.

At least it was a response, and that was what she hoped for.

"It is obvious you have never lost anyone you loved deeply," he reproached her.

"But you know that I have. Both my mother and my father are dead."

"But you never wanted to stop living!"

"I didn't?"

Jerome was riled. "Well, if you did, then tell me—tell me how you got through it!"

"It took a long time. I think I wanted to hold on to my grief—wanted to strike back at life, but that was before I came face-to-face with Jesus Christ. He had a purpose and a way for me to go."

"How does one get back to living again, Maryetta? Life cannot ever be what it was. If you know the way, for God's sake, tell me!"

"It is true, Jerome. It will never be the same, but life does go on. Someday you will discover that God can heal—and give us reasons for all that is difficult in our lives."

"I can't see any sense to life or any reason to live."

"The most important reason is out there in my kitchen."

"I don't spend any time with her now. She would never even miss me."

"How blind you are! Do you want her to spend her life wondering why you didn't love her?"

Jerome studied Maryetta intently. "Why do you care so much about her?"

Maryetta looked away from the piercing eyes. Then she spoke, as much to herself as to Jerome. "Because . . . I was that child. I know what she is feeling. I know where she will find herself. I know. . . ."

Jerome recalled the disillusioned young girl who had given him a rose at a Brussels concert and asked him to pray for her. He sank wearily into a chair and covered his face with his hands.

Maryetta reached out and touched his shoulder ever so lightly, and suddenly he was sobbing like a small child.

She waited without speaking until his weeping subsided.

"Where do I begin?" he asked, looking at her from red eyes.

"Your music."

"I don't seem to want to play anymore."

"Try it. Arrange for concerts. Go back to Europe."

"And Elise?"

"I will keep her for the rest of the winter. Ellen and I would love to have her, and she can visit Bethia and her grandfather whenever she likes."

Jerome was listening. "I would pay you, of course."

"No. I would ask only one thing."

"Anything!"

"I would ask for a promise—two promises. First, that you make no lifetime commitments for five years. And second, that when you do, you allow Elise to share in such decisions."

"That is a strange request."

"I have observed that a man in your situation can be very vulnerable to designing women. He can make mistakes."

"If you mean marriage, you can rest assured there will never be another woman in my life."

Elise came into the room with Ellen. Jerome seemed to see her for the first time in months.

"Come here, Elise." He placed his arms around her. "Would you like to live here with Maryetta and Ellen for a little while?"

Elise ran to Maryetta. "May I?" she asked.

"Yes," said Maryetta with a tender smile. "I think you may."

23

Toward the end of April Maryetta heard the Haddons' old wagon pulling to a stop just outside her door. It was still cool enough for hot chocolate, and Ellen hurriedly put some to heating on the stove as Maryetta went to the door to welcome Bethia.

There was something new in the beautiful blue eyes and a certain spring to her step.

"You have something to tell me," said Maryetta at once.

"How did you know?"

"One has only to look at you, Bethia. You are all aglow."

"Drake has asked me to marry him! Oh, Maryetta—I thought he would never ask."

"Tell me about it." Maryetta set down her sewing to listen.

"I brought him a pie—I've always done that—and, as usual ended up cleaning his kitchen. It was in such a state. I guess I was fuming—told him his place needed a woman. I suggested he look around at all the young girls who would be glad to marry him."

"You didn't name them," Maryetta said facetiously.

"No, but he asked me if I would like the job."

"He's a rascal!"

"I told him I did not love him enough to put up with his ridiculous ideas."

"You lied."

"Yes, and he knew it."

"And he kissed you."

"How did you know?" Bethia asked again.

"It's all over your face!"

Bethia grinned. "We shall be married in the fall and live in the house he built on Father's land—where I have always wanted my house to be. I always said I would have a 'prophet's chamber'—a room for hurting people—and now we'll have it together!" Bethia's face was rapturous.

"Mercifully, our grief is healing, and God is blessing." She continued, "Father and Allen have grown very close. I always have thought that Allen should have been my father's son, he is so much like him. He keeps believing that Timothy will come home some day—I admire his trust and his faith.

"And you—you have changed a lot, Maryetta. From the poor frightened little European creature who first came in at the train station, so insecure and alone . . . you are now a grown woman full of peace and security."

"Yes, I have found my answers. I believe the purposes of God are to make us servants and give us our own sphere of ministry. Many of my dear friends in the past tried to teach me that, but I wasn't ready. They had found their purpose and their niche. Now I have found mine.

"But what of you? When do we get together to sew your wedding finery?"

BY JUNE the weather had settled and flowers and trees had reached full bloom. Jerome would be coming any day for his daughter, and Maryetta had packed Elise's small trunk. She was looking forward to the joy on the child's face when her father came to say he was taking her on a brief summer cruise before returning to the Boscowen farm.

Jerome arrived at her door via the old depot wagon.

Watching Elise run into his arms brought quick, hot tears to Maryetta's eyes. Always, it seemed, Elise was filling up the years Maryetta had lost.

Still kneeling with his arms around his daughter, Jerome looked toward Maryetta.

"Elise has grown!" he managed with some abashment. They entered the sitting room, Jerome still with his arms around Elise.

"She is looking more like Caroline all the time, isn't she?" he commented.

He looked like the Jerome Cavell she had first met at the Brussels concert hall.

"You will stay for lunch?" asked Ellen, heading for the kitchen. "We have fish chowder and common crackers. Come along, Elise, you can help."

"Sounds like New England! Sounds good!" said Jerome.

Maryetta inquired about his European concerts.

"My patrons remembered me—I was welcomed back."

"Did you take the teapot I gave you to Sister Florence at the convent?" she asked, smiling.

"Yes, I delivered it in person to your sister. She was very pleased." Jerome shook his head. "I never thought I'd see the day when the progeny of a Huguenot would be taking a gift to a Catholic nun."

Maryetta laughed. "Won't heaven be wonderful, Jerome—when we can chuck all our preconceived ideas? All the man-made regulations and rules, denominational barriers, hatreds, and biases will be gone, and we'll just sit down together at the feet of Jesus!"

Jerome was listening, entranced. "Yes, Maryetta, heaven grows more precious with the passing of time. It is as you said—I do value my memories and can look forward to seeing my Carrie again—my grandmother, too."

"But to see the King of Glory!" exclaimed Maryetta, her face aglow. Then she was back to the moment.

"I almost forgot—we have something to show you." She made her way to the parlor piano and opened it.

"Come, Elise!"

Elise came into the room displaying a childish grin. She took her place on the fringed piano stool and began to play a simple nursery rhyme tune. Her tapered fingers, longer than the usual seven year old's, stretched naturally for the chords.

Jerome's face brightened as he watched—his heart in his eyes and approval on his lips. When she finished, he pulled a chair up beside her and gave her his own instructions.

"See—this way. Music tells a story—you must tell it with feeling!" And he demonstrated an octave higher.

Elise was observing closely and approached the keys again, duplicating exactly what she had seen and heard. This done, she hopped down from the stool and ran back to the kitchen.

"Ellen, Ellen! Guess what! My own father just gave me a lesson!"

Jerome chuckled, but sobered, too.

"How can I ever thank you, Maryetta Cobbet? You have done so much—given me back my life and now—Elise. How did she get interested in the piano?"

"I caught her at it repeatedly. She started by picking out simple tunes, some she had learned in church and some I had taught her. But she was using the wrong fingers, and I couldn't let her do that! So I gave her lessons. She took to learning like a deer to high land."

Ellen announced that lunch was ready, and they gathered around the table.

"You say grace, Father," said Elise.

And he did so with genuine sincerity.

MARYETTA DID NOT SEE JEROME and Elise again until Bethia's fall wedding.

"Allen didn't come?" Jerome asked as he stood beside Maryetta, looking over the guests at the reception.

"He is a little depressed. Seems one of his old friends ran into Timothy in Colorado. He didn't want to talk to him—actually he avoided him."

"But there will come a day—there will be healing," said Jerome optimistically.

"You have discovered that."

"Yes, thanks to you."

"And Elise—have you enjoyed your summer together?"

"We have kept on with the lessons. I think Elise has the makings of a performer."

"Caroline would be so proud."

"I can't thank you enough." The dark eyes were serious and filled with gratitude.

Maryetta, always uncomfortable receiving praise, quickly changed the subject. "And you, are you keeping your head—and your promise?" she asked.

"About making no commitments for five years?"

"Yes."

"Well, I may ask you to release me from that promise before the five years are up."

"Well, I won't do it!" said Maryetta firmly. The gray eyes were more serious than were her smiling lips.

"I think—perhaps—you might!" said Jerome, lifting her hand to his lips and returning the smile.

ABOUT THE AUTHOR

ONCE AGAIN JANET BEDLEY reaches into the past to bring to her readers the sequel to her first novel, *Promises Broken, Promises Kept.* Janet says, "the people of our illustrious nation's past were not only flesh and blood people, but strong enough of purpose and character to set this country on a path of unparalleled accomplishment and glory at the very heart of their decisions, labors, and dedication lay the solid rock of the Christian faith." She endeavors to build her novels on that sure foundation and to challenge the young generation to learn of their courageous forebears.

Janet started writing children's stories for her child evangelism classes, which she taught for over thirty years. She credits the encouragement of her grandfather and her access to the Newburyport, Massachusetts Library where she served as head librarian for fifty years, as the spark that started her on a literary career.

Janet lives with her husband, Robert, in the San Bernardino Mountains of California. She is the mother of five grown children.